"You ... to demonstrate."

Eliot was going to kiss her and Fleur wanted him to. But she couldn't risk it.

"There's only one reason for marrying, I believe, and that's if two people are in love. As you and I certainly aren't in love, it would be simply for . . . for convenience. And sex," she added. She could hear her voice trembling. Damn it, she'd been congratulating herself on handling this situation with poise. Now she'd spoiled it.

His blue eyes were full of mockery and . . . something else that she couldn't put a name to.

"Dear little Fleur," he said. "I won't try to win you round to my way of thinking tonight, but I warn you, I'm not going to give up the idea."

Marjorie Lewty is a born romantic. "It's all in the way you look at the world," she suggests. "Maybe if I hadn't been lucky enough to find love myself—in my parents, my husband, my children—I might have viewed the world with cynicism." As it is, she writes about "what is surely the most important and exciting part of growing up, and that is falling in love." She and her family live in Leamington, a pleasant town full of beautiful parks and old Georgian homes.

Books by Marjorie Lewty

Don't miss any of our special offers. Write to us at the following address for information on our newest releases.

Harlequin Reader Service
901 Fuhrmann Blvd., P.O. Box 1397, Buffalo, NY 14240
Canadian address: P.O. Box 603,
Fort Erie, Ont. L2A 5X3

Bittersweet Honeymoon
Marjorie Lewty

Harlequin Books

TORONTO • NEW YORK • LONDON
AMSTERDAM • PARIS • SYDNEY • HAMBURG
STOCKHOLM • ATHENS • TOKYO • MILAN

Original hardcover edition published in 1988
by Mills & Boon Limited

ISBN 0-373-02985-3

Harlequin Romance first edition June 1989

CHAPTER ONE

'JUST a minute—please wait——'

The girl's clear voice echoed off the stone walls of the narrow covered passage and her sandals clicked on the worn, uneven flagstones as she sprinted along, tawny curls lifting in the chilly breeze that always blew sneakily through the passage from the quay, even on a warm September day like this one.

The tall man in the dark suit was almost at the end of the passage now, just before it turned a corner to emerge into the main street of the little Cornish town. He paused and glanced briefly over his shoulder. Then, not seeing anyone he recognised, he strode on again.

'Stop!' yelled Fleur, and—taking a chance that it was the man Caroline had said it was—'please stop, Mr Stevens.'

He stopped then, only half turning, frowning as she covered the final twenty yards at a gallop. 'Yes?' he questioned, not particularly courteously.

Fleur came to a halt before him, breathing rather fast, partly because she had been running quickly, but mostly because she was feeling slightly nervous—an unusual feeling for Fleur, for whom shyness was no problem. 'You're Mr Stevens? Of Stevens Constructions?' Oh, lord, how *big* he was now that she was close to him! In the dimness of the covered passage he seemed to loom over her like a dark, threatening figure from a nightmare.

'Yes.' Black brows lifted. He wasn't troubling to conceal his impatience.

Fleur tried to marshal her thoughts. When Caroline had murmured, 'That's him, now! That's the Stevens man—why don't you go after him and ask him?' Fleur hadn't stopped to think—she'd rushed impulsively out of the shop and down the passage after the man striding along ahead of her.

And now, confronted with this intimidating individual, she searched wildly for the best words in which to ask her question.

Glittering dark eyes raked her from top to toe and evidently dismissed her, in her jeans and green cotton top, as a shop-girl and of no conceivable importance to him. 'Well, what is it, then?' he barked. 'Go on, girl, get on with it.'

Arrogant brute! Fleur swallowed her quick anger; it was no use antagonising him. 'I'm Fleur Gold, Mr Stevens—from the florist's shop on the quay-front.' She waved a slender brown arm in the direction she had come from.

The tall man made a dismissive gesture. 'Look, Miss—er—I'm already late for an appointment, and——'

'I won't keep you a moment,' Fleur interrupted. Now she had started, she had no intention of being brushed off. 'I've just been told that your company has bought the building, to turn it into a club or something and that—that our lease isn't going to be renewed. Would you please tell me if it's true?'

She felt, rather than saw, the man's cold annoyance. His voice cracked with ice as he said, 'I don't make a habit of discussing business in the street. I suggest you tell your proprietor to take up the matter of the lease with his solicitor.' He turned away and began to walk on.

What an absolutely hateful individual, Fleur fumed inwardly. Oh, but she would like to puncture that outsize ego of his. Lifting her nicely rounded, stubborn, small chin, she went after him. 'Mr Stevens—*I'm* the proprietor—or rather, my mother is, and she's away at present. And it's not a discussion—I'm asking for a yes or no, that's all. It's the weekend—Saturday tomorrow—and I won't be able to find out anything definite until Monday. If I've got to spend two days worrying, not knowing, I'll—I'll go crackers,' she ended up, biting her lip as the childish term slipped out. *'Please.'*

She grabbed the arm of his grey, fine-wool jacket as he turned the corner, and he came to a halt again with a grunt of exasperation. For a moment she thought he was going to shake her hand off, but instead he stood glaring down at her as she drew herself up to her full five feet six. In her casual jeans and top she looked younger than her twenty-two years and she knew it. Usually she didn't much care but, facing this intimidating man, she longed for more inches and more years to be able to meet him on his own ground.

In the narrow shaft of sunlight that found its way in from the street and shone across the ancient stone walls of the passage, Fleur looked up into the face of the man before her and wasn't reassured by what she saw. Oh, he was handsome, in a sexy, saturnine way, but his eyes had a dangerous glitter and his mouth was a straight, hard line. Not a man to tangle with. In spite of her righteous indignation, something that felt like fear gripped her stomach. Her hand that was holding his arm felt weak and powerless and she stared down at it help-lessly, quite incapable of moving it. Beneath the sleeve of his jacket she could feel muscle like steel wire. There was nothing unbending about this man, he was tough all through. Her heart sank like lead. She could have saved herself the trouble of appealing to him; she wasn't going to get an answer.

Then, to her surprise, the straight mouth twisted into a cynical smile as he looked down into the small face framed by its cap of tawny curls; a face with large, troubled green eyes and cheeks that were pink with annoyance.

'As I said, I don't discuss business in the street,' he said, 'but if it's the only way to get rid of you without getting rough, little girl——' he glanced down at her hand on his arm '—I'll make an exception in your case. The answer to both questions is yes. And now, if I may be allowed to go on my way——?' he added, his voice heavy with irony.

'Of course. Thank you,' Fleur muttered. Little girl, indeed! Patronising beast, she thought furiously. Her hand dropped to her side as he strode away and turned the corner without a backward look.

She leaned against the rough, cold stone of the wall, knees shaking. It was like being punched in the stomach—worse, because the bombshell about the lease was so utterly unexpected and the Stevens man had rammed home the bad news with such cold lack of feeling that the bitterness of resentment was added to her dismay, and left her feeling empty and quaking inside.

Presently she pulled herself together and began to walk very slowly back along the passage, drawing aside to allow a school party to trail past, hooting enthusiastically, laughing in delight as the echoes travelled back to them along the covered way.

It would all go, Fleur thought despairingly, the old building with its odd, unexpected passage cutting through the middle. The bulldozers would move in and the grey, massive stones that bore the scars and salty encrustations of hundreds of years would come crashing down to make way for some smart club with restaurants and bars and swimming pools and jacuzzis and all the other amenities the rich sailing set expected.

That was bad enough, but much, much worse—how was she going to tell her poor, gallant mother, when she got back from her holiday with Aunt Brenda in Miami, that the little shop she loved so much was going to be swept away when the lease expired in a couple of months' time? Fleur's throat tightened as she remembered her mother's white, tired face at the carriage window of the London train last week. It hadn't been too difficult, in the end, to persuade her mother to accept Aunt Brenda's invitation. The gritty energy that had stood Janet Gold in such good stead all through the difficult years of widowhood, when she had brought up her daughter alone, had suddenly seemed to flag when fate had dealt her a new and crushing blow, when her second marriage had ended so tragically in a crashed car in a narrow Cornish lane, just five weeks ago.

Fleur had gone straight to Cornwall from London when it had happened, having just finished her final year at university. She and her mother had always been close and she knew that her own love and compassion had helped through those first harrowing days. But she had been desperately worried when, afterwards, Janet threw herself back into the work of the flower shop with a kind of hectic energy.

'Take it easier, Mum,' Fleur had pleaded after a couple of weeks, as the colour faded from Janet's cheeks and the spring went out of her step. She was only forty-three, but suddenly she looked ten years older. 'You'll wear yourself out. Give yourself a break—I can manage the shop, with Betty to help me.'

For once, perhaps, fate had been on Janet's side, for it was then that the invitation from her sister Brenda had arrived, together with an airline ticket to Miami and a dire and affectionate warning that Brenda positively refused to take no for an answer.

'You must go, Mum,' Fleur had urged. 'You haven't seen Aunt Brenda for ages, and it would do you the world of good.'

Janet pushed back a straying lock of fair hair wearily. 'I don't know if I should go away, love. You know how much it's meant to me to have you here with me, but you've got your own life to think of. And there's Roger——'

'It's not serious with Roger and me,' Fleur lied quickly. She wasn't going to tell Janet just how serious it had been with Roger—on her side, at least. And she certainly wasn't going to tell her about the wounding letter she'd had from Roger yesterday, because she couldn't trust herself not to burst into tears if she did. If Janet knew that Fleur was feeling miserable and let-down she would refuse point-blank to go to Miami, and Fleur had determined that she should go.

'Oh, well——' Janet was weakening, Fleur could tell. 'It *would* be lovely to see Brenda again. But—there's all the monthly accounts—and the Templeton wedding next week, and——'

'I can do the accounts on my head,' Fleur offered confidently. 'Ditto the wedding. I haven't been practically brought up in a flower shop for nothing. I can decorate the church and make up a bouquet with the best of 'em, as you well know. I won't let you down, and I'll have Betty to help. You go, and have a good rest, then you can come back feeling more fit to tackle things again.'

Her mother wasn't the weepy kind, but now her eyes filled with tears. 'It's very dear of you, Fleur, love. I'm silly about the shop, aren't I? I've longed to have my very own shop for so many years and I love it so much. And Tom bought it for me as a wedding present. Somehow it feels like a sort of—of memorial to him to make a success of it. If I didn't have it I'd feel horribly lost and lonely.'

'You're not——' Fleur began to protest, but Janet went on,

'Oh, I know what you're going to say. You're going to say that I've got you. I know I have and you're a darling girl, but you have your own life ahead and I *refuse* to lean on you.'

Fleur grinned wryly. 'I've leaned on you plenty over the last twenty-two years.'

'That's entirely different—that's what a mother's for, to be leaned on—for a time at least.' A ghost of Janet's old impish smile flickered. 'So I think I won't go to Brenda's, kind though it was of her to invite me. I'll stay here and look after the shop and you can start your job-searching. There now, that's settled.'

Fleur looked at her mother in silence. Then she firmed her pretty mouth. 'It isn't settled, you know, Mum,' she said, very slowly and very quietly. 'You *are* going. And I shall look after the shop for you. So don't argue.'

Janet pulled a face, her eyes still misty. 'You and Brenda,' she said. 'Terrible bullies, both of you.'

That conversation passed through Fleur's mind like a warning of impending doom as she retraced her steps slowly along the passage. How would her mother take this new disaster? Hadn't she had enough trouble in her life without yet another blow, so soon after the last one that had nearly wrecked her? What can I *do*? Fleur asked herself, biting her lip in desperation.

The florist's shop was on the corner, the tiny front window overlooking the quayside, with its bollards and ropes and lobster pots, its piles of netting and unmistakable smell of tar. The entrance to the shop was in the passage itself, and opposite to it, on the other side of the passage, was the door of the almost identical small shop where Caroline Dunn sold her jewellery—some of it Victorian, some handmade by Caroline herself, working in the dark little cubby-hole behind the counter.

Caroline was waiting as Fleur returned, her pretty, usually cheerful face pulled into a frown of anxiety. 'Well?' she asked, looking hard at Fleur. Then, 'No, I can see it's *not* well.'

Fleur walked into the shop and sank on to the chair put there for customers. She shook her head. 'Couldn't be worse,' she said, pursing her lips grimly. 'You were right, Caro, he's going to pull it all down and build a beastly sailing club.'

Caroline clapped a hand to her forehead. 'Oh, lord, that's bad. It doesn't matter so much for me, I'll be getting married soon anyway, and Johnny doesn't really want me to keep on the shop, but it's wretched for you, Fleur. I know how you feel about your mother and she's worked so hard here, building up the business and everything. It's such a perfect place for a flower shop. It's going to be hard to find anything else as good.'

She was right, of course. No other shop—even if they could find one to rent—would be so right. Fleur looked around, her eyes misty. The delicate blooms—rosebuds, carnations, freesias, the pottery bowls spilling over with violets, the bunches of garden flowers, lupins and delphiniums and marguerites and golden anthemis, that she had so lovingly arranged this morning in their water-containers, glowed like jewels against the grey stone of the walls, and their mingled perfume hung sweetly on the moist, cool air. The little shop was like an Aladdin's cave of colour and beauty, tucked away here beside the quay, where late holiday-makers strolled, and took photographs, and sat around on slatted wooden benches in the September sunshine.

'What did he say?' asked Caroline. 'What was he like?'

Fleur's lips drew together. 'He said almost nothing, I had to practically go down on my knees to make him listen to me at all. He simply confirmed that he *had* bought the building and intended to turn it into a sailing club. Then he walked off without another word. Horrible man! A chauvinist of the first order, our Mr

Stevens. Overbearing, condescending—I could—could——' Fleur's hands formed themselves into fists and angry colour ran into her cheeks.

'Good lord—you were only with the man about thirty seconds. He *must* have made an impression!' Caroline chuckled mischievously. 'Johnny pointed him out to me yesterday in the Planning Department, and I thought he looked a rather gorgeously sexy number.' Then she was quickly serious again. 'Sorry, Fleur, I know it's no laughing matter. What will you do? Will you write and break it to your mother now, or——?'

Fleur shook her head worriedly. 'I can't. I had a letter this morning and she says she's feeling so much better; I really think she's enjoying being with Aunt Brenda in Miami. She says America's such a huge, exciting place that it seems to make your own troubles seem smaller, and that she's going to work hard at making a new life for herself when she gets home again. She's got all sorts of ideas for expanding the business here—perhaps extending the shop into the empty room behind and selling pottery and craft things. It's such a damn *shame*,' she added fiercely, her eyes filling with tears.

The other girl nodded in quick sympathy. 'I know, that's how I felt when Johnny told me about it last night.' Caroline's fiancé, Johnny Bains, worked in the Planning Department in Truro. 'He wasn't sure that it was definite—perhaps I shouldn't have told you when I saw the Stevens man walking past.'

'I'm glad you did,' Fleur said shakily. 'When there's bad news I like to hear it and get it over.' She blinked the tears away, staring through the window between the banked flowers at the ruffled water of the harbour where fishing-boats rocked at anchor and gulls wheeled and swooped against the cloudless blue of the sky. 'I'd like to strangle all property developers,' she burst out, 'and Mr Superior Stevens most of all. Oh damn, damn, damn! It looks as if the Templeton wedding tomorrow will be our first and last big order.'

'Will you look for another shop?' Caroline asked.

'I suppose we'll have to. But even if there's a vacant one anywhere in the town—which I don't think there is—I should guess the rent would be three times what we pay here. Anyway, that'll have to wait for the moment. I've got to go up to the Templetons' now to report finally on the flowers for the church and the bouquet, and from what Mum told me about Mrs Templeton she would *not* be amused if I turned up late. Would you be an angel and hold the fort for me until Betty arrives, Caro?' Betty, who helped in the shop, cycled in from a nearby village, and her time-keeping was somewhat erratic. 'The prices are all in the book, except for those little pot-plants—the parlour palms— and they're one pound fifty. Right?'

'Right, will do,' Caroline agreed amiably, and Fleur stuffed her order book into her tote-bag, hitched it over her shoulder and set out for the car park, her small face determined and resolute. Whatever happened, the flowers for the Templeton wedding must be a success.

She had been up very early this morning to clean and polish the van. It stood out among the visitors' cars, immaculate with its glossy green paint and the neat white inscription, 'Porthgurran Flowers', on its side. She touched the bonnet lovingly before she unlocked the door and climbed in. Everything, this morning, had seemed to be more hopeful: the increase in cash takings last week, the wedding order from the Templetons who lived in the big house up on the cliff, the letter from her mother who seemed actually to be turning the corner at last, after the grief and shock.

Even her own wretchedness about Roger's letter had seemed to be lifting a bit; perhaps it was because she had come to a decision, in bed last night, to stay here and help Janet in the shop and not look for a teaching job—at least, not for the time being. Between them they would make a success and perhaps open other shops, bigger ones, in the towns—Truro, or St Austell. Her head had been full of plans.

But when Caroline had arrived, with her rumour about the lease, all the pleasure had gone out of the day. And that beastly Stevens man had made everything worse, if that were possible. She let in the clutch with unaccustomed clumsiness and the van jerked violently before she backed it round and drove out of the car park, along the busy main street, past the new bungalows, and took the U-turn into the steep lane that led to the Templeton house.

As the little van tackled the four-in-one gradient Fleur changed down into second gear. The house stood by itself, high on the grassy cliff-top, surrounded by at least an acre of garden and a paddock. It was an imposing house, long and low and stone-built. John Templeton was 'something in the city' and only appeared here at intervals, and Fleur knew that the family was not very popular with the local residents. 'Stuck-up furriners,' was the verdict that came from the post-office-cum-general-shop. Fleur was always glad that she couldn't be considered a 'furriner', for Janet, her mother, was Cornish born and bred.

Which was why she and Fleur had come back to Cornwall for a summer holiday last year, before Fleur began her final year at university, and it was here that they had met Tom Lind, the manager of the local bank, a widower with an attractive cottage just outside the small town. He and Janet had fallen in love and a month later were married, and Fleur was delighted that at last her mother should have a good life for herself after all her years of widowhood and unselfish struggle.

Such happy hopes and plans Tom and Janet had had. Janet had managed a florist's shop in Birmingham for years, supporting herself and Fleur, and had always wanted to have a shop of her very own. Tom, indulgent and loving, had bought the little florist's business on the quay for her when the previous owner left the district, and Janet was over the moon with pleasure. Fleur had spent her last Easter holiday from college with her mother and her new stepfather, and helped her mother in the shop, as she had often done during her growing-up years. She loved flowers, and her slim, nimble fingers could wire a wreath or make up the sun-ray ribbon trimming for a gift sheaf as deftly as could her mother's. They were so happy, working here together in that Easter holiday, and she got on so well with her new stepfather, that she was almost tempted to skip her final term and make her home here and work in the shop.

But of course there was no real future for her here, and anyway she could never forget how Janet had worked and skimped to bring her up alone, to buy her pretty clothes, and help out with her education. Fleur loved her mother dearly and felt that she owed it to her to do as well as she could for herself. So she kissed them both, a little tearfully, and got on the train back to London at the end of the Easter vacation.

That was the last time she saw her stepfather. The very day that Fleur finished her final exams, a telephone call from her mother's neighbour told her that her stepfather's car had been involved in an accident on one of the narrow Cornish lanes, and that he and the other driver had both been killed.

Fleur sighed heavily now, gripping the steering wheel as the van chuggered over the rough grass track that led to the entrance to the Templeton house. Her mother was such a darling; she didn't deserve such bad luck. There must be some way that she could keep the flower shop that she cared so much about, in spite of that beastly Stevens man's beastly plans. If there *was* a way then she, Fleur, would find it, she vowed stubbornly. Perhaps she could get up a petition or something. Caroline's Johnny might explain the legal position. And there was the solicitor, Mr Banks, he might help——

As she parked the van in the wide drive, well away from the large array of cars and vans already parked there, Fleur had to drag her thoughts back to the matter of the moment, the Templeton wedding. She mustn't let her mother down. The wedding had to be a success—from the floral point of view, anyway.

The garden was a hive of activity. One gardener was mowing carefully parallel stripes on an already smooth lawn. Another was on his knees, weeding an already immaculate rosebed. Several workmen were shouting to each other as they struggled to put up a huge marquee.

It was going to be a very grand wedding indeed. Fleur felt rather relieved that she wasn't going to be responsible for the decorations here. Flowers for the house and the marquee, her mother had explained, would be provided from the Templetons' own garden.

She climbed the stone steps and rang the bell and the imposing front door was opened by a dignified elderly man wearing a green baize apron. Butler? Footman? 'About the flowers, miss? Ah, yes, Mrs Templeton is expecting you. Will you wait in the morning-room, please?'

Fleur followed him across a square hall and into a long room, heavy with dark antique furniture. Here she waited for twenty minutes, sitting uneasily on an uncomfortable brocade winged chair. This wasn't a room, or a house, that had any appeal for her, and the sooner her business was concluded the better.

She got to her feet as Mrs Templeton came into the room. She was a tall, fashionably bony woman with a high colour, only partially concealed by the layer of foundation that covered her cheeks. Her blonde hair was cleverly streaked and cut stylishly short, and a pale mauve lacy twin-set and pearls was obviously intended to establish its wearer as 'county'.

'Good morning, Mrs Templeton,' Fleur began, smiling pleasantly. 'Thank you for your phone message. I'm sorry my mother can't be here to see you; she has to be away from the shop for a time, but she has attended to all the ordering herself and I'm sure I shall be able to handle the church arrangement and the bouquet to your satisfaction.'

'Away from the shop? What do you mean—away from the shop?' Mrs Templeton's thin eyebrows rose. 'Affronted' was the only word to describe her tone of voice. If she had been wearing a lorgnette she would certainly have raised it as an expression of her displeasure, Fleur thought, suppressing a giggle.

'My mother hasn't been very well,' she explained, 'and her doctor ordered a rest. She has gone abroad for a holiday.' Not the precise truth, perhaps, but near enough.

'Well!' The woman's pale eyes fixed on Fleur as if she were a specimen of some lower order of life. 'This is most unsatisfactory. Most annoying. I placed the order with your mother's shop because I wished to support local tradespeople, and this is the way I'm treated.' She was beginning to work herself up into a temper. 'As if I hadn't enough to do without *this* on top of everything else. I certainly didn't expect the flower arrangements to be handled by a chit of a teenager!' she added nastily.

Fleur pulled herself up to her full five feet six and looked the woman straight in the eye. 'I'm twenty-two, Mrs Templeton. I'm experienced, and I'm perfectly confident that I can handle your order to your complete satisfaction.'

Mrs Templeton ignored her as if she hadn't spoken. She tapped a silver pencil petulantly against her reddened lips. 'Well, I suppose I shall just have to get on to a florist in Truro and see if they can take on the work at short notice.'

Fleur began to seethe inwardly, but she must remain cool, whatever provocation she received. 'That's as you wish, of course, Mrs Templeton,' she said smoothly. 'But I must draw your attention to the fact that we have your

signed order and the flowers you chose will be delivered
to us this afternoon. I'm afraid we shall have to hold
you responsible for the agreed payment.'

Mrs Templeton's cheeks flushed a darker shade of red.
'Why, you——' she began. Then the implication of
Fleur's words began to sink in. With an exclamation of
disgust she waved a hand, dismissing the whole matter
as beneath her contempt. 'Very well, then, if that's your
attitude you must do the best you can. But I shall be at
the church tomorrow morning at ten o'clock to see what
you're doing,' she added sharply. 'And the bouquets and
posies must be delivered here in good time in case they
are not satisfactory. I must say—why, Eliot, my *dear*
boy, come in.'

The change of tone was startling, like pouring honey
into a glass of vinegar. Fleur turned her head, and when
she saw the man standing in the doorway her stomach
gave a small jolt. What ghastly luck to encounter the
Stevens man twice in the same morning! He was leaning
nonchalantly against the doorpost, and now that she saw
him in full daylight she had to admit that Caroline had
something when she described him as 'rather gorgeous'.
The eyes that Fleur had taken for black in the dimness
of the passage were actually blue, she saw now, the
deepest blue imaginable. His grey jacket sat perfectly
over broad shoulders and the close-fitting trousers that
covered his long legs hardly seemed to conceal the strong
muscles beneath. Yes, her first impression had been
correct. He was certainly a dominant male with a very
good opinion of himself. He carried his sexiness with a
confidence that might, just possibly, be unconscious but

probably wasn't, Fleur decided contemptuously. The kind of man she always steered very clear of.

'Good morning, Sheila.' He sketched a bow in Mrs Templeton's direction. 'Am I interrupting something?'

'No, no, nothing important at all. How are you, Eliot dear, all ready for the big day tomorrow?' Mrs Templeton almost simpered as she tripped across the room to him and held up her cheek for a kiss. 'Lovely to see you—have you driven down from London or come by train? Melissa will be thrilled. The dear girl is upstairs, having a few final touches put to her dress. Of course you *mustn't* see her in it.' She smiled archly at him. 'It's always bad luck for the groom to see the bride in her wedding-dress before she joins him at the altar.' She trilled with girlish laughter. 'Or is that being foolishly superstitious?' More trills. 'You'll have lunch with us, of course?'

'Well, actually, I've arranged to take Melly out for lunch. I'm sure you're much too busy to bother with me.' The man came a little way into the room and his glance fell on Fleur. She saw the way his brows lifted a trifle and felt a flicker of surprise that he had recognised her.

He turned back to Mrs Templeton, who was assuring him fervently that it would be no bother at all, but of *course* Melissa would *love* to go out to lunch, and they would have *lots* to discuss about the honeymoon, wouldn't they? 'I'll tell her you're here, Eliot, it will be a nice surprise for her.' She walked past him to the door and called, 'Melissa—Melissa, darling, guess who's here!' Silence. 'She can't hear me with the bedroom door closed. I'll go up. Pour yourself a drink, Eliot, do.' Mrs Templeton disappeared from sight into the corridor.

She seemed to have forgotten Fleur's presence entirely, and Fleur turned to the door. The sooner she got away from this house, the better; it certainly wasn't her scene.

The Stevens man was lounging against a mahogany table, in her direct line to the door. 'Excuse me.' Fleur paused, not looking at him, waiting for him to step aside.

He didn't move. 'Well, well,' he murmured. 'If it isn't the little flower-girl.'

She looked up at him then. It seemed a long way up. 'Professor Higgins, I presume?' she said coldly. She hadn't played a small walk-on part in Shaw's *Pygmalion* for nothing in her final year at college.

The dark blue eyes flashed momentarily. 'Not Eliza Doolittle, though? Fleur Gold, I seem to remember.'

'Correct,' Fleur said crisply. Surprising that he should remember, but then he was the type of high-powered executive who cultivated an encyclopaedic memory for names. 'May I pass, please?'

'Of course.' He stood aside and Fleur stalked past, her bright head held high.

He took a couple of steps after her and held open the door, which had swung to after Mrs Templeton's exit. 'Miss Gold——'

'Yes?' Fleur stopped. Could he—could he possibly be going to say something about the shop? Something that might reassure her, if only a little? She looked up into the brilliant blue eyes and her inside churned with a faint hope, and some other feeling that she couldn't put a name to.

'I was going to congratulate you on the way you held your own with Mrs Templeton,' he said, his long mouth twisting in amusement. 'It was quite a polished performance. Although perhaps you didn't get your facts right. The bride's mother may have ordered the flowers, but I understand the groom pays for them.'

Fleur was too surprised to reply. She hurried past him to the door and almost collided with Mrs Templeton, returning. Behind her, drifting down the stairs, was a girl in a white, filmy négligé.

'Melissa—my sweet! You look marvellous.' The Stevens man strode eagerly towards the staircase, put his arms round the girl and lifted her down the last two steps. 'Glad to see me?' He kissed her slowly, with unashamed enthusiasm.

'Oh, Eliot—please!' The girl drew out of his embrace, her cheeks pink.

Fleur hesitated, standing aside in the doorway, feeling faintly embarrassed but hardly able to take her eyes off Melissa Templeton. She had never seen her before, so far as she knew, but that was hardly surprising—they didn't move in the same circles. But she had heard the local gossip, which reported that she was a pretty girl who was completely under her formidable mother's thumb.

'Pretty' hardly described her, Fleur thought now. She was classically lovely. Pink and white and with a dreamy, ethereal look about her. Long, shining, white-gold hair framed an angelic, heart-shaped face. Huge, limpid blue eyes gazed up at her fiancé with a slightly dazed, out-of-this-world expression. An odd expression that Fleur couldn't put a name to. She was like a Botticelli angel,

Fleur thought, and much too fragile for a great hulk like the Stevens man, who was gazing hungrily down at the girl as if he could eat her.

'Run up and change, my love,' he urged, 'and we'll get going. I've booked a table at a special little pub I know on the river. I think you'll like it.'

The girl looked from him to her mother, who was standing gazing fondly at the two of them. 'I was going to see Miss Barnes about my head-dress,' Melissa said timidly.

'Oh, I'll see to that,' Mrs Templeton waved away her daughter's hesitation. 'Now, you two young love-birds run along. Hurry up and dress, Melissa.'

The girl turned slowly towards the stairs. 'I'll come and help you,' the Stevens man said, smiling.

'Oh, no!' Melissa said sharply. 'No.' Her cheeks had paled.

'Why not, my sweet? We're getting married tomorrow, remember?'

'No, you mustn't,' the girl said again confusedly. Then, hurriedly, 'My wedding-dress is hanging up in the bedroom. You mustn't see it before tomorrow. It would be bad luck.'

Eliot Stevens sighed tolerantly as Melissa ran up the stairs, her white négligé floating behind her like a cloud, but Fleur, who was watching this little scene, fascinated, saw his face darken.

Mrs Templeton looked up at her future son-in-law with a rueful little smile. 'Pre-wedding nerves! Don't take any notice.' She linked her arm with his. 'Come along, Eliot dear, and I'll pour you a drink.'

Fleur thought Mrs Templeton had forgotten all about her and now she moved forward from where she had been standing, half-hidden by the open door. 'If there isn't anything else——?'

The woman gave her a dismissive glance. 'Nothing more. Just remember what I said.'

'I will, Mrs Templeton,' Fleur said, making for the front door. Oh, yes, I'll certainly remember what you said; I just hope I'm going to be able to stop myself being really rude to you, as you deserve.

The sight of the tall, dark man with the woman hanging on to his arm, fluttering a smile up into his face, was the last thing she saw as she went out to the van. They made a good pair, she thought, and felt a little sorry for Melissa Templeton, that fragile girl who was likely to be crushed into oblivion between those two dominant personalities.

Poor Melissa, she thought. It was none of her business, of course, but as she drove back to the shop down the steep hill she put a name to the expression that she had seen on the girl's face as she looked up at her husband-to-be, and it certainly wasn't love. It was fear that looked out of those huge blue eyes. Sheer helpless panic.

Which wasn't surprising. The prospect of marriage to a man like that would be daunting to any girl, let alone a sweet, delicate girl like Melissa Templeton. She wondered if pressure had been put on her by her mother to agree to the marriage.

But marrying Eliot Stevens was Melissa's problem. Her own problem was still looming before her. Her brow was creased in deep thought as she parked the van in the car park and walked slowly back through the passage to the shop on the quay-front.

The Stevens man would be away on his honeymoon after tomorrow. That would give her some time to try to find a way out. She'd go to see the solicitor first thing on Monday morning.

Somehow—she gritted her teeth—somehow she was going to stop that beastly, superior man from high-handedly stepping in and spoiling something good that her mother had worked at so hard and lovingly.

Anger simmered inside Fleur again as she remembered the way he'd drawled, 'Ah, the little flower-girl!' It set her teeth on edge just to recall his voice and the amused, condescending way he'd looked down on her from his much greater height.

He'd tried to—to *diminish* her, and she wasn't going to forgive him for that. He had posed a threat to her self-image. Her fists clenched. On all counts he was the enemy, and if there was any way to be found—any weapon she could use—she was going to fight him.

Fleur could hardly have guessed, when she made this dramatic vow, that a weapon would be put into her hand so soon.

CHAPTER TWO

'THE vase to the left of the altar steps—a little further forward, I think, Miss Gold.' Mrs Templeton, in stylish trousers and a tailored silk blouse, stood at the communion rail, one perfectly manicured finger beside her mouth, considering the floral decorations in the small Norman church.

Fleur gritted her teeth and moved the vase of white phlox and stephanotis an inch forward. She had been up since six. The bouquet, the posies, the corsages, the buttonholes—all made and delivered. After that, hours of work in the church, and now Mrs Templeton had arrived to give her grudging approval, after a few pernickety alterations—a twitch of a bloom here, a spread of a misty arrangement of maidenhair fern and gypsophila there.

'Yes, I think that will do. Do you agree, Vicar?'

'Indeed I do. Well done, Fleur. You've made the old church into a bower of beauty. Your dear mother couldn't have done better.' The vicar, a small, cheerful man, was an old friend and had been a rock of comfort to Janet after the tragedy.

There were evidently no congratulations coming to Fleur from the bride's mother. A job had been done and would be paid for, and praise was in short supply.

'Yes, I think my choice of colours was the right one.' Mrs Templeton half turned her back on Fleur, waving

28

a graceful hand towards a display of white and palest yellow rayonnante chrysanthemums that Fleur had placed on the niche where once the ancient north door had stood. 'I do like plenty of white at weddings. So delicately pure and virginal, don't you think, Vicar? Especially in these disgracefully lax days.' The thin lips twisted fastidiously.

'Oh, yes, indeed.' Over Mrs Templeton's shoulder Fleur met the vicar's small, twinkling eyes and had an idea that they were twinkling even more than usual behind his round glasses.

Mrs Templeton's high heels tapped on the tiles as she marched down the aisle. 'Well, I must hurry home to dress now. Always so much to be seen to at the last minute! And my dear girl to be supported—such a sensitive child, needs a great deal of help and encouragement!' She bestowed a dazzling smile on the vicar as he caught up with her at the church door. 'Goodbye for the present, Vicar. We shall meet later, of course, and we shall be delighted to see you at home after the service. Just a small luncheon to toast the happy couple. Eliot Stevens is such a wonderful man, as I'm sure you agree, and so successful for a man of his age. My husband and I are delighted with Melissa's choice.'

The vicar bowed. 'Thank you, Mrs Templeton. I shall be pleased to come.'

Mrs Templeton's pale blue eyes moved briefly to Fleur, who had followed the other two to the door. 'I expect you will like to come to the church, Miss—er—Gold. I imagine there will be room in the back pews.' She hurried importantly to her car and drove away.

Fleur turned to the vicar. 'Well!' she exclaimed, with meaning.

The little man gave her a wry look. 'Your reward will be in heaven, my dear Fleur,' he said, and they exchanged an understanding smile. 'Shall I see you in church later?'

Never, thought Fleur, as she drove her van back to the shop. The thought of seeing Mrs Templeton in all her wedding finery made her feel slightly sick. And, as for Eliot Stevens, she would prefer to see him being led away to jail in handcuffs rather than being married to that frail, exquisite girl, Melissa. No, she certainly wouldn't go to the church.

Which made it somewhat surprising that two hours later Fleur, in a pretty, flower-sprigged dress, found herself half-hidden behind a pillar in a side pew, watching the guests arrive. Curiosity had brought her here, she supposed, and the pleasure of admiring her own floral arrangements. The old church certainly looked its best, with sunlight flooding through the stained glass to lend a mysterious beauty to the grey stone pillars and the carved bench-ends and the delicate masses of flowers over which she had taken such loving care.

The guests must be nearly all here by now; the front pews were full of expensively dressed women and men in morning suits. Outside, the September sun shone brilliantly, but inside the church was blessedly cool and French perfume drifted on the air, mingling with the scent of freesias. Well-heeled friends and relations of both the bride and the groom, most likely, Fleur thought; certainly not local people. From where she sat she could get only glimpses of the front pews. Mrs Templeton's hat was plainly visible—an elegant model affair in black straw, with a wide, stiff brim in the shape of an enormous dinner-plate. She was whispering to an older, white-haired woman sitting next to her and they both looked back over their shoulders towards the west door.

Across the aisle from them Fleur could make out the dark head of the bridegroom, and next to it that of his best man. Their two heads made a stark contrast—the bridegroom's black as night, the other man's golden as a summer cornfield. They were chatting together, the bridegroom leaning towards the man beside him. Not seeking reassurance, Fleur was sure. You couldn't im-agine Eliot Stevens being nervous, even on his wedding day. She looked away quickly. Even the sight of the back of that man's head made her nerve-ends prickle.

Minutes passed. No more guests were arriving now. The organ continued its rather wandering Bach prelude, half drowned by the powerful sound of the church bells, as the ringers put on a spirited performance for the happy occasion.

Fleur glanced at her watch. Brides were always a little late, of course, it was their privilege, but Melissa was stretching it a bit, surely? Fleur could see the young bridesmaids, in their frilly primrose-yellow dresses, fidgeting in the porch. The smallest, a little girl of about three, was dancing up and down, bored with the inac-tivity, clutching her lilies-of-the-valley so tightly that Fleur feared for the dainty little posy she had made early this morning.

Time was dragging now, each minute longer than the one before it. The congregation was definitely growing uneasy. Murmurs swelled, heads turned, service sheets rustled, and the air seemed to buzz with questions. 'Where is she?' 'What has happened?' Fleur glanced at her watch and saw that it was almost half-past twelve.

Suddenly there was a stir in the front pews. The vicar appeared and was immediately deep in conversation with Mrs Templeton. Then he moved across and spoke to the bridegroom. A buzz of conversation passed like a wave through the congregation, and, as heads turned to follow, Mrs Templeton walked rapidly down the centre aisle to the west door where the bridesmaids were waiting. Her smoothly made-up face was blank, her pale blue eyes stared straight in front of her. After a moment or two she was followed by the vicar.

Fleur's eyes went to the dark head of the bridegroom. It was fixed, motionless. Unlike everyone else, he was not looking back towards the door from which his bride should by now have appeared on her father's arm. After a moment she saw him stand, lean down to speak to the yellow-haired man beside him, and then walk rapidly across the nave towards the vestry.

Abruptly the bells stopped pealing and after the joyous clangour their silence was somehow ominous. The organ continued doggedly, but the sound became hesitant and after a few more moments that, too, ceased and in the silence that followed the congregation seemed to be holding its breath. The vicar's steps sounded loud on the tiled floor as he paced heavily back as far as the chancel steps and then turned to address the congregation.

'My dear friends.' His usually cheery face was grave. 'I am grieved to have to tell you that the wedding arranged for midday will not now take place. You will no doubt be glad to hear that this is not due to illness or accident. Mr and Mrs Templeton deeply regret disappointing you all, but they would be most relieved if you would return to the house, as arranged, to partake of lunch. You will, I am sure, excuse the family themselves if they are not present to meet you.' He bowed his head and murmured something that might have been a short blessing.

Fleur sat where she was while the congregation drifted out of the church; she had no wish to mingle with the wedding party. So—the lovely Melissa had escaped, and Fleur wished her well. She didn't suppose she would ever know the details herself, but she couldn't help a sneaking feeling that the odious Eliot Stevens had got what he deserved.

Everyone had left now except for the warden and the bell-ringers. Not wishing to get involved in a guessing session about the missing bride, Fleur hurried out and cut across the grass of the churchyard to where she had parked her van in a narrow lane near the side door of the church. She had left Betty in charge of the shop, with instructions to close for the day at one o'clock. It seemed hardly worth while going back there, so Fleur decided to drive home to the cottage for lunch. Later, perhaps, she would return to the shop and clear things up for the weekend.

The cottage stood by itself at the end of a long, straggling lane a couple of miles from the small holiday town. It had once been two cottages and had been completely converted and renovated by Tom Lind some years ago when he took over at the bank. He had been delighted to give his new wife a free hand to make any changes she liked to the furnishing and decorations, and the result was a home of charm that might have featured in a glossy magazine. Fleur couldn't return here without a slight lump in her throat when she remembered all Janet's pleasure in the planning: in choosing new curtains and covers and buying all the small additions that there had never been enough money to buy during the lean years of Fleur's growing up. Tom had been delighted and so proud of his new wife, after many years of living a solitary life. Oh, why did it have to end so soon? Fleur asked herself for the hundredth time as she pulled up the van in front of the cottage. They had been so happy together——

She switched off the engine and walked round to open the back door of the van to get out the flowers she had brought home from the shop. It was Janet's habit never to sell flowers that weren't absolutely fresh, and the remainder either came home or went to the hospital. Today there had been a large bunch of pink roses to bring home, and they would look lovely in the sitting-room when she had given the cottage its weekly clean and polish. If she kept busy it would perhaps stop her worrying fruitlessly about the matter of the lease. There was nothing she could do about it until she saw the solicitor on Monday morning.

She pulled open the double doors of the van, put one foot on the step and nearly fell over backwards.

Inside, seated on the floor, hugging the knees of long legs encased in grey striped trousers, sat Eliot Stevens, the forsaken bridegroom.

Fleur's first reaction was blazing anger. How *dared* he make use of her van in this way? She glared at him balefully, her green eyes sparkling in the midday sunshine.

'What the hell are you doing here?' she demanded.

He glowered back at her. 'What does it look like? I'm taking an afternoon stroll, of course.'

Fleur pursed her lips, which had dropped apart in surprise. 'Well, you can't take it in my van,' she said. 'Get out.'

He shook his head. 'No way. Not until it's dark.'

'Don't be ridiculous,' Fleur said crossly. 'You can't sit here for another six or seven hours.'

He gave her a very nasty look. 'And who's going to stop me?' He locked his hands more firmly round his knees.

Fleur regarded his twelve stone odd of hard, muscular masculinity doubtfully. 'I could call the police.'

He must have heard the slight hesitation in her voice for he changed his tone. 'But you won't, will you, Fleur? I can see you're a girl with a kind heart. You'll do me this small favour, won't you?'

Tables turned! Now *he* was doing the pleading.

'The name is Miss Gold,' she said crushingly. 'And why should I do you a favour? You're certainly not my favourite person. I haven't noticed that you're exactly co-operative yourself.'

But even as her wrath simmered she couldn't help noticing how absolutely shattered he looked. His black hair was standing in spikes where he had raked his fingers through it. The dark blue eyes were half closed and there were tight little lines between them, and a whiteness round his mouth.

His wide brow creased and he pushed back a stray
lock of hair impatiently. 'What——' he began. Then,
'Ah——' as light dawned. 'Yesterday morning, by the
quay—I was in a hurry.'

'You were very rude.'

He groaned. 'OK, OK, so I was very rude. I apolo-
gise. Now, be a good girl and go away and leave me to
my escape.'

'Escape?' A shiver passed down Fleur's back. He
wasn't a criminal, was he? Was *that* why Melissa hadn't
turned up at the church? Had she suddenly discovered
that he was on the run from the police? Her thoughts
buzzed round her brain like wasps round a honey-jar.
'Wh-what are you escaping from?' she stammered, her
mouth dry. As if he was likely to tell her!

He hitched himself up further against the side of the
van and in so doing dislodged two bunches of pink roses
from the top of a cardboard packing-box. 'Ouch!' He
sucked a finger. 'These damn things bite.'

'Roses usually do,' Fleur informed him coldly.

'So I've observed, Miss Gold.' He gave her a narrow,
meaning look, and to her horror she felt the blood rush
into her cheeks. 'As to escaping—no, I'm not being
pursued by the law.' Damn him, he had read her mind.
'I'm escaping from a mixed assortment of wedding guests
slavering for scandal. But principally I'm escaping from
Melissa's mother, who's on my trail. I only just made
it in time when I leapt into this——' he looked around
at his cramped quarters '—this flowery sanctuary.'

Then, as if he was at the end of his tether and he
didn't care who knew it, he dropped his head on to his

knees. 'I just have to get away from the whole bloody scene,' he muttered. 'I have to.'

Fleur's eyes softened as they rested on the dark, bent head, and impulsively she stretched out a hand. Immediately she snatched it back again. What was she thinking of?

'Well,' she said practically. 'You can't sit here for hours. For one thing it's my day for cleaning out the inside of the van. This is my home.' She jerked her head towards the cottage. 'You'd better come and wait inside then and I'll make some coffee.'

His head shot up and he peered along the empty lane behind her. The nearest cottage was fifty yards away, hidden behind high bushes.

'Don't worry,' said Fleur. 'You won't be seen and there's nobody here—I'm on my own at present.' The thought that she was being unwise to invite a strange man into the cottage passed through her mind and out again. Instinctively she knew that in the circumstances Eliot Stevens posed no threat.

He was looking at her as if he couldn't believe what he was hearing. Then the ghost of a smile touched the corners of his mouth. 'Bless you,' he said. He uncoiled his long legs and followed Fleur up the front path into the cottage.

She threw open the door of the sitting-room, glad that she had tidied it up before she left this morning. Not that Eliot Stevens would notice, in his present condition. She waved towards a plumply cushioned armchair. 'Do sit down,' she said courteously. She was hostess now; wisely or not, she had invited him into her home, and

the rules of hospitality which her mother had always observed came naturally to Fleur.

'Would you like coffee?' she asked, as he sank into
the chair.

'Thanks, that would be nice,' he said wearily. Then,
as she turned towards the door, 'I suppose—you
wouldn't have any whisky about the place, would you?
I'm feeling a trifle bushed, if the truth were told.'

'I think there's some.' On her way to the sideboard
she glanced at the man in the chair. He looked awful,
ghastly pale and tense. It must be the worst thing that
could happen to a man—to be humiliated as he had been.
For the first time she felt a twinge of disapproval towards
the absent Melissa. Surely she hadn't needed to let him
down quite so brutally? She thought briefly of Roger—
at least he had been civilised about ending their relationship—well, reasonably so. She pushed away the
thought of Roger—she was determined not to wallow in
self-pity. Life had to go on, and there would be someone
else for her eventually—but not for some time yet. She'd
had enough of romance for the present.

'My stepfather always kept a bottle of Scotch here
somewhere,' she muttered, rummaging in the cupboard.
'Ah, here it is.'

She pulled up a small table and put the bottle on it,
then fetched a glass and a jug of water from the kitchen.
'Help yourself,' she said.

She stood watching while he poured out a stiff whisky
and tossed it down, then repeated the process. He looked
up and saw her still standing there. 'Don't worry,' he
said, 'I'm not going to get drunk. This is just to blunt

the edges. And I'll buy your stepfather another bottle of whisky. Two bottles. Three.'

Fleur felt relieved. For a moment she had feared that she was going to be landed with a visitor who was tipsy as well as unwelcome. 'My stepfather's dead,' she said, turning away. 'I'm going to make some sandwiches for my lunch. Do you want some?'

'Thanks,' he said vaguely, leaning back and closing his eyes.

Fleur wasn't quite sure whether he had taken in what she had said, but she made a hefty pile of cheese and tomato sandwiches, just in case, and two mugs of black coffee. If the sandwiches weren't all eaten she could wrap the remainder up in cling-film and put them in the fridge. Or give them to the birds. She had never quite got over the frugal economy that had been a necessary part of her childhood.

She carried the tray back to the sitting-room and put it on the low table, removing the whisky bottle. Eliot Stevens opened his eyes and stared at her as if he were trying to remember who she was. Then he saw the tray and pulled himself up.

'Sorry,' he said, 'I'm being rather a drag. This is very kind.'

'That's all right,' Fleur said. 'I was going to eat, anyway.' It was stupid, but suddenly she felt unusually shy and awkward. Hastily she gave him a plate and pushed the sandwiches towards him. 'I've made the coffee black,' she said. 'Is that OK?'

'Excellent,' he said politely. 'Just what I need.'

They ate and drank in a stiff silence, and Fleur felt more and more embarrassed. Usually she had no trouble about chatting to anyone and everyone, but this was different. What could you offer in the way of small talk to a man who had just been left at the altar? He wouldn't expect sympathy from her. She stole a glance at him over the rim of her coffee-cup and met his eyes, watching her.

'When did your stepfather die?' he said.

Fleur blinked. 'Just over a month ago,' she told him. He could hardly be interested. He was probably making conversation to take his mind off his misery.

'And you live here on your own?'

'Oh, no, it's my mother's home, but she's away at present and I'm here looking after the house and the shop for her.'

He helped himself to another sandwich. 'Ah, yes, the shop. You said something about it yesterday when we—er—encountered each other.'

Fleur's resentment of yesterday surfaced again. 'Yes, I did,' she snapped. 'And you made it quite plain that you didn't want to know.'

'Did I? Well, I'm listening now. Tell me.'

She eyed him suspiciously. He didn't look, or sound, in the least bit interested. But she couldn't miss an opportunity that fate, or whatever, had handed to her. Not that she expected any joy from an appeal to Eliot Stevens, but at least this was a chance to put her case to him when he wasn't likely to get up and walk away.

She took a long swig of black coffee and said, 'I'd just heard that your company has bought the old building on the quayside and that the leases of the two small shops that front on to the quay were not going to be renewed. I was upset and worried because the florist's shop is my mother's and she—she loves the place. She's not been well since my stepfather's death in a road accident, a few weeks ago, and she's gone away for a rest. I—I couldn't bear the thought of confronting her with bad news like this when she gets back. You were pointed out to me, when you walked past the shop yesterday, as the owner of the company who had bought the building so——' she paused '—so I ran after you to ask whether the rumour was true.'

'And I told you it was.'

'Eventually—yes,' said Fleur shortly.

Putting down his coffee mug, he regarded her in silence, his face closed. Meeting those dark blue eyes, cold as the harbour water, Fleur felt a strong urge to argue, to fight with him. The faint pity she had felt for him a few minutes ago was forgotten. No man had ever roused her antagonism so thoroughly in such a short space of time. 'It doesn't matter,' she said. 'I don't suppose anything can be done about it. That's progress, isn't it?' she went on bitterly. 'Pulling down lovely old buildings to put some modern horror in its place.'

His gaze moved slowly over her face, taking in the curling tawny cap of hair, the angry light in the green-grey eyes, the straight little nose, its slight tip-tiltedness giving the lie to the general belief that firm decisiveness goes only with a large nose. Fleur could be very firm, if necessary. And at the moment the upward tilt of her nose, together with the downward curl of her soft lips, registered scorn and disdain.

To her annoyance the man didn't take up the argument. 'Oh, I wouldn't say nothing can be done about it,' he said mildly. 'I don't believe in ever giving up easily.'

'That's Big Business speaking. What would you suggest my mother and I do?' Fleur flung at him, getting more heated as he refused to be provoked. 'Organise a two-woman demonstration? Lie down on the quay in front of the bulldozers?'

He was actually smiling faintly now, and Fleur felt a small shock of surprise. He had, for the moment, forgotten about Melissa, about his aborted wedding. He was giving her his full attention.

'That conjures up an intriguing picture,' he said. 'It's quite a pity it won't be necessary. We haven't any plans to bring the bulldozers in. Apart from some necessary repair work on the masonry, we don't intend to alter the outside of the building at all, nor remove that rather fascinating passage through the middle of it.'

'You don't?' Fleur said blankly.

'We certainly don't. Wouldn't dream of it. The inside, of course, is a different matter.'

Ah, thought Fleur, now we're coming to it.

'The inside,' said Eliot Stevens, 'will have to be completely gutted—except for some of the load-bearing walls, of course. It's pretty well falling down already. Most of the building's empty now, except for the big hall at the back, at present being used as a sort of weekly market, and the two shops at the front—your mother's and a little holiday gift place.'

'A jewellery shop,' Fleur corrected loftily. 'A friend of mine sells hand-crafted jewellery there.'

'A jeweller's if you like,' he said indifferently. 'But as I've just told you, the inside of the place is in a very bad state. It would probably start to crumble away in a few months anyway, left to itself. Surely you've noticed the water running down the walls?'

Fleur *had* noticed. The damp atmosphere of the shop helped to keep the flowers fresh. It had seemed to her to be somehow in keeping with the rest of the building. Old buildings by the sea were probably always damp, she had registered, without really considering the matter.

'So, I'm afraid your mother's lease won't be renewed,' he went on. 'But we haven't yet got down to final plans for the reconstruction. It might be an idea to——'

He broke off, stroking his chin, his face thoughtful. Fleur held her breath. Was it possible that he was going to suggest that the shop might be contained, in some way, in the new lay-out of the building? She didn't dare speak, or ask him what he had been going to say.

Then he said abruptly, 'Oh, well, it's all in the future,' and she saw that he had lost interest in the matter.

In silence she stood up and gathered the plates and mugs on to the tray. She said stiffly, 'I bring the books and paperwork home on Saturday, so I'll get on with it. Naturally you won't expect to be entertained, Mr Stevens.'

'Hm? Oh, yes, of course. I mean no.' He looked up at her vaguely. Then he squeezed his eyes up, shaking his head as if he were trying to shut out some picture in his mind. 'Thank you for putting up with me,' he added.

'That's all right,' Fleur said, a little awkwardly. 'I suppose I'm——'

'Sorry for me?'

'Well, in a way I am, though I don't expect you'd want pity from a stranger who knows nothing about the circumstances.' She was still holding the tray and now she turned towards the kitchen. 'No, I suppose it's a kind of fellow-feeling.'

'Fleur——' An odd note in his voice stopped her. 'Put that tray down and come back,' he said. 'I need someone to talk to or I'll start downing the rest of that bottle of Scotch, and you wouldn't approve of that, would you? You can do your books tomorrow, when I've gone.'

She took the tray into the kitchen, then she came back and sat down in the chair opposite him. He had his head buried in his hands, and when he raised it to stare bleakly into her eyes he looked so utterly wretched that she guessed that the full reality of what had happened had only just struck him—the knowledge that his lovely Melissa wasn't going to be part of his future. Like having an accident—you don't feel the pain immediately.

At last he said between his teeth, 'I love her, you know—I love Melissa. I'm crazy about the little fool.'

'She's very beautiful,' Fleur ventured, feeling her way carefully. It was like treading over a minefield must be.

'She's perfect—damn well perfect. Her face—her body—oh, God,' he groaned. 'What a thing to happen— what a bloody awful thing.' He drew his hands down his cheeks, lifting his face to the ceiling.

Then he lowered it and stared at Fleur, but she didn't think he was really seeing her. 'It was her mother's doing—that bitch of a woman——' he bit out the words.

'But——' began Fleur. She was going to say that Mrs Templeton had seemed to be thrilled about the wedding.

He suddenly thumped his fist on the table. 'Hell—I don't want to think about it—or her—or any damned thing—it's all so bloody awful——' He slumped back in his chair, his eyes closed.

There was a long silence. Then he opened his eyes. 'Tell me about yourself, Fleur. Fellow-feeling, you said. Tell me about it. Talk to me.'

Fleur looked into the drawn face of the man sitting opposite. She could understand that he needed desperately to take his mind off what had happened; she remembered the sick shock she had felt when the letter from Roger arrived. Then, to her surprise, she heard herself telling Eliot Stevens about it.

'Nothing dramatic—just an ordinary little episode,' she said, biting her lip hard, because it hadn't been ordinary at all to her. 'I expect that's how most girls would see it—the ones who change their boyfriends every few weeks anyway. But it wasn't like that with Roger and me, at least I didn't think it was. He was three years older—he'd come back to college to take his PhD. We met at a college dance and—and after that we saw a lot of each other. I—fell in love with him. He said he felt the same about me.'

She looked out of the window, trying to see Roger's face—the light brown, crisp hair, the teasing eyes that squeezed up when he laughed, the square chin with the slight cleft. She could remember all that, but she couldn't *see* him. Perhaps, she thought, her heart lifting a fraction, she was getting over him, something that she had thought could never, never happen.

'Go on,' said Eliot.

'Well—it was the end of the year at college. We'd both finished our courses. Roger had a teaching job lined up in Yorkshire. We'd planned that I'd go up there too and try to find a job, and if things worked out we'd get married. Then my stepfather was killed in a car accident and I came back here straight away to be with my mother. She was absolutely shattered—they'd only been married a few months and they were very much in love. It was a——' she choked over the inadequate words '—a beastly shame.'

'What happened to your own father?'

'I never knew him; he died when I was a baby. My mother's been coping on her own all these years. That was why—you see—I was so anxious to find out about the lease of her shop. It means such a lot to her, and if she comes home and finds that she's going to lose it it will be a very bad blow to her, when she's trying hard to adjust to what has happened.'

'I see,' Eliot said and she glanced at his face, wondering if she could possibly have touched a chord of sympathy, if a miracle might happen and he might arrange something so that Janet could keep the shop. But his expression told her nothing.

'And what about Roger?' he asked, and her heart fell as he changed the subject so pointedly.

She shrugged. 'He went up to Yorkshire—he took another girl with him. He wrote to me, saying he was sorry but as I was so—"tied up with my family" was the way he put it—he didn't think it would work out. I suppose he was right. From Yorkshire to Cornwall is a long way, and I couldn't possibly just walk out and leave my mother on her own—not for a while, anyway. I couldn't expect Roger to wait for me.' She turned her head away, biting her lip hard.

Eliot pushed himself out of the chair and walked over to the window, hands stuck deep in his trouser pockets as he stared out. Fleur struggled with her tears, gulping silently until she had control of herself again. It was the first time she had told anyone about Roger; certainly she couldn't have told her mother what had happened—not at present. And it was odd how talking about it seemed to have helped. She felt lighter, more free than she had felt for days. It was even more odd that it was Eliot Stevens in whom she had confided—a man who was a complete stranger and whom she didn't even like.

She looked at the tall back in the formal wedding-suit as he stood at the window. The black morning-coat and grey striped trousers fitted impeccably; his bronzed neck was strong above the rim of white collar, his dark hair healthily luxuriant. There was no doubt, Fleur thought detachedly, that he was a strikingly attractive man. She wondered just what had happened to make Melissa walk out on him. And why he seemed to lay the blame at Mrs Templeton's door, when that lady had been so jubilant about the wedding. Ah, well, she would never know. Certainly he wouldn't be moved to confide in her as she had confided in him.

He turned and came back to his chair, leaning forward, and for the first time the deep lines had smoothed them-selves from his forehead. 'You know,' he said, 'I believe I may have found a partial solution to our problems, yours and mine.'

Fleur just stared at him.

'Have you got a valid passport?'

He shot the question at her so quickly that she replied, 'Yes—why?' before she had time to consider her answer.

'Good, that's the first step. You know, it's quite extraordinary how our situations parallel each other in a strange sort of way. Let me explain. My father lives in Italy—he went there when he retired and now his health is—poor. He's always been very keen on the family thing—carrying on the name and the business he founded, and so on. As I'm an only son, that seems to be up to me. I'd arranged my——' his face hardened '—my honeymoon to be spent near my father's home so that I could take—Melissa—to see him. So that we could spend some time with him. Now——' he shrugged '—you see my problem?'

Fleur nodded. If he cared so much about his father he was more human than she had thought. But what did he mean about a 'partial solution'?

'I don't dare to think how my dad will take it if he knows what has happened,' he went on. 'The housekeeper who looks after him says he's very frail. I spoke to her on the phone a few days ago and I was troubled by what she told me. She said he's been living for our visit, counting the days. I think he's afraid he won't last until——' He broke off, looking away from her for just a moment. Then he turned back and his blue gaze was fixed keenly on her. 'Do you see what I'm getting at?'

'Frankly, no,' she said, but somewhere at the back of her mind the seed of an idea was stirring uncomfortably.

'Let me put my suggestion as baldly as I know how. You accompany me on my honeymoon, playing the part of my wife for my father's benefit. In return, I promise to safeguard your mother's claim to transfer her flower shop to the new building. It would be a solution for both of us.'

The glittering dark blue of his eyes seemed to be having a hypnotic effect on Fleur. Was she dreaming, or was this really happening? He leaned forward and covered her hands with his, and his touch sent a curious tingling up her arms and made her heart jolt uncomfortably.

'What do you say, Fleur? Is it a deal? Don't you think I've come up with a brilliant suggestion? Now, suppose we get down to discussing the details?'

CHAPTER THREE

FLEUR almost exploded. The arrogance, the sheer gall of the man, taking her for granted like this! 'You're not serious?' she gasped.

'Certainly I am. As I said, it seems a wonderful answer to both our problems.'

Green eyes flashed angrily. 'It doesn't seem wonderful to me. It's quite impossible.'

'Why?' he said calmly.

The perfect example of the high-handed male chauvinist! Fleur's feminine dignity revolted violently. She beat both her fists on the arms of her chair. 'Why?' she flung at him. '*Why?* I should have thought it was obvious. To go on a honeymoon with you—to pretend to be your wife, when I only met you half an hour ago—I don't count yesterday—when I don't know the first thing about you. No,' she fumed, indignation sending hot blood rushing into her cheeks, 'we certainly can't make plans. It's a ridiculous idea. How could I possibly act as your wife? I've never acted in my life, and anyway, I——' she met those gleaming dark blue eyes in angry challenge '—I don't even like you. We're poles apart.'

He watched her narrowly. 'But there's a spark between us, haven't you noticed? And *I* would be playing the leading role. I shouldn't find it hard to convince anyone that I'm in love with you, Fleur. You're a very pretty girl.'

'Thank you,' she said distantly. She got up and stalked into the kitchen.

He followed her. 'Please consider the idea, at least. It really would be an act of human kindness on your part. You're a kind girl, I know that.'

She threw a plastic bowl into the sink, turned on the tap with a rush of hot water and squeezed out far too much washing-up liquid. 'Pretty! Kind! Aren't you being rather obvious with your flattery, Mr Stevens?'

'I hope not.' His deep voice, coming quietly from behind her, reverberated in her head. 'It's the truth. And think what a relief it would be for both you and your mother. Fun, too, for you to be in on the ground floor in the new building work. You could have custom-built premises to your own design.'

'Bribery,' Fleur muttered, grasping a mug and plunging it into the foaming white mass of suds.

Eliot was standing close beside her now. He picked up a tea-towel and dried the mug absently as she clattered it down on the draining-board. 'Not really bribery. It's the only weapon I have, so I must use it in a good cause—the best. My father means a very great deal to me—always has. Now,' he added wryly, 'go on, accuse me of emotional blackmail.'

She turned and met the challenge of those brilliant blue eyes and her breath caught in her throat. Then she said slowly, 'No, I won't accuse you of that. I believe you. But——' she moved a little away from him '—it wouldn't work.'

Her mind was spinning, passing over half a dozen things at once and getting hopelessly mixed up.

There was an oddly taut silence while between them they washed and dried the remainder of the lunch dishes. Then he said, 'There wouldn't be any strings attached, you know, if that's what's bothering you. I'm in no mood for dalliance.' His voice was suddenly harsh as he added, 'Surely you can understand that?'

Fleur recalled the look on his face when he had seen Melissa walking down the stairs towards him. A look of hungry adoration. Oh, yes, she could well understand that she herself would be no substitute for his lost love.

She lifted her chin. 'That *wasn't* what was bothering me, Mr Stevens,' she said coldly. '*I'm* certainly not in the mood for any—dalliance—either.' After Roger she was going to be very careful—very choosy.

'Well, then——' he said.

When she hesitated, her hands moving vaguely in the bubbles of detergent, he took a towel off its hook, held it out to her and said, 'Dry your hands and come back and sit down. There's something I want to show you.'

Fleur looked round for an excuse to refuse, but there was nothing to be done in the kitchen. It was all clean and tidy. She dried her hands, not hurrying, not giving him the satisfaction of knowing he had aroused her curiosity, walked back to the sitting-room in a dignified silence and sat down.

He took the opposite chair again, reached into an inside pocket of the black morning-coat and drew out an envelope. 'I'd like you to read this,' he said, taking a single sheet of notepaper from the envelope. 'It came this morning. It's a letter from my father.'

Fleur's hands clenched and she shook her head obstinately. 'No, I can't read your private letters.'

He still held it out towards her. 'Read it,' he said.

His eyes were so piercingly blue; she had never before seen such intense blue eyes. Slowly her hands unclenched and fell limply to her lap. The hand that went out and took the letter from him felt as if it didn't belong to her.

The handwriting was thin and spidery, and the words were inclined to run off the end of the lines.

'My dearest boy,' Fleur read. 'This should reach you in time for your wedding, and how I wish I could be there. But you know how I shall be thinking of you and counting the days until you bring your beautiful little bride to meet me. It seems so strange that I've never even seen your Melissa, but it will be all the more delightful when I do finally meet her, and hear all the little details that your somewhat rambling and lyrical short letters have left out! Dear old boy, you know how much your happiness means to me, Your loving Dad.

'P.S. The doctor is determinedly cheerful but I don't feel too chirpy, I fear. *But* I'm determined to stay alive until your visit!!!'

Fleur handed back the letter. 'He sounds—nice.'

'He *is* nice.' Eliot held the sheet of paper in his hand for a moment, his eyes passing over the uneven writing, and his face was unreadable. 'Very nice.' Then he folded the sheet slowly and replaced it in the envelope.

'How ill is he?' Fleur asked.

He drew in a tight breath. 'Difficult to say, but I'm not too hopeful. He had a heart attack about six or seven months ago, a short time after they retired to the south. The doctors say he's partly recovered and he can lead a fairly normal life, but he doesn't seem to be able to bring himself to believe them. The trouble is, he seems to have lost interest in everything, and when a man like my dad loses interest in life—well——' He shrugged.

'You said "they". Isn't your mother with him? Can't she rally him?'

Eliot's lips drew together. 'That's most of the trouble.' He hesitated for a moment, then went on, 'Oh, well, you know so much, you may as well know the lot. It might help you to make up your mind. My mother died when I was a baby and my father married again soon after—to a much younger woman. The marriage had been rocky for some time, I knew that. When my father decided to retire and go down to Italy to live—which was what my stepmother said she wanted—he hoped they could pull things together. But it didn't work. After a couple of months she walked out. A week or two later he had his heart attack. It was a——' he drew in a tight breath '—a bad time.'

He got to his feet, paced to the window, then came back and sat down again. 'Now do you see why I said that in a curious way our difficulties seemed to parallel each other? Why it occurred to me that we might be able to help each other?'

Fleur's eyes searched the face of the man sitting opposite. It had great strength, she knew that already. The wide brow, the long, slightly crooked nose, the firmly moulded chin, all spoke of a hard, possibly ruthless character to whom making decisions and carrying them out were the breath of life. But when he spoke of his father there was a tenderness in his face which redeemed it from coldness. Yesterday she had resolved to pay him back for his high-handed treatment of her. It was ironic, she thought, that now she had a weapon she couldn't use it. But oh, how wonderful it would be to save Janet's flower shop!

'All right,' she said. 'I'm willing to discuss your idea. But I still doubt if it would work.'

He leaned forward, deep blue eyes searching her face. Then he held out his hand. 'We'll make it work. It's a deal, then. I promise to keep my side of the bargain.'

Fleur put her hand in his. His hand was warm and dry, and there was an intensity in his grip that took her by surprise. She hadn't been prepared for the hot rush of blood that flooded through her body and into her cheeks—the response of a woman to a man's inborn sexuality. She must ignore that passing weakness. Looked at from any angle, this was a risky thing she was agreeing to do, and she certainly mustn't complicate it by falling for a man who, less than half an hour ago, had told her he was crazy about another girl.

They spent all afternoon making plans—at least, Eliot made plans and Fleur listened, only breaking off to go into the kitchen and make tea and butter scones. Pouring out tea somehow made things seem marginally more normal.

Eliot kept looking towards the telephone, and he jumped visibly when it rang. But it was only Betty, saying that she had locked up the shop and would be late coming in on Monday morning because she had to call at her sister's to take a jacket her Mum had knitted for the baby.

Fleur replaced the receiver and glanced at Eliot's fingers, drumming nervously on the arms of his chair. 'You *are* jittery, aren't you? I promised you sanctuary here.' She came back to her chair, not looking at him as she said, 'Though I really don't see why you need to hide yourself away.' That wasn't a very subtle way of discovering what she wanted to know, and she didn't really expect him to rise to the bait.

He didn't. He relaxed again and returned to what they had been talking about. 'Well, that's the plan, then. We wait until it's dark, then take your van out to the church, pick up the hired car with my bag in it, drive to the station and catch the night train to London—I've got reservations booked. From then on we follow my original plan for the honeymoon. We stay at my flat tomorrow and on Monday we fly from Heathrow to Nice. I'm buying a new car from a dealer there and he'll be at the airport when we arrive to hand it over. Then we'll drive to San Remo, which is over the border into Italy. I've made bookings at a hotel there. It's not far from where my father lives.'

He slid a quick glance at Fleur as she drew in a breath to speak. 'Don't panic, I've booked two rooms—at Melissa's request. She insisted that she needed lots of space for all her clothes and her dressing arrangements.' Neither his face nor his tone of voice betrayed any emotion, and Fleur guessed that he was being deliberately matter-of-fact about it. Like touching a sore place to see how much it hurt. She knew the feeling.

'Any questions?' he said, holding out his teacup for a refill.

'Several,' Fleur said coolly.

He sat back, sipping his tea leisurely. 'Shoot,' he said.

'Well, first of all, I think you should tell me why you're so desperately keen on avoiding everybody. Why all the cloak and dagger business of waiting until it's dark, and stealing away in the night and so on?'

He was silent, looking down at his hands, the long, bony fingers spread out on his knees. 'I suppose,' he said slowly, 'that you could put it down to a basic animal instinct to hide away and lick one's wounds. Added to which, if I saw Melissa's mother just now I wouldn't be responsible for my actions.' He glanced up at Fleur. 'You've met Mrs Templeton yourself, haven't you? She's the one who's to blame for the whole ludicrous performance at the church today.' His mouth twisted bitterly.

'But—but——' Fleur couldn't help saying what she had previously been thinking '—Mrs Templeton was thrilled to bits about the wedding and about having you as a son-in-law. You could see that. I don't understand——'

He moved his shoulders impatiently. 'You don't have to understand,' he said curtly, 'and I don't want to talk about it.'

Fleur felt her cheeks go warm at the snub, but she supposed she had invited it. And, although it still seemed extraordinary that Mrs Templeton should be responsible for what had happened, Eliot had made it quite clear that it was a taboo subject. Unless she was prepared to accept that, she must here and now refuse to consider his plan further.

That was what she should do, of course. Common sense warned her against entering into such a crazy scheme, even though a refusal would mean her mother's losing the beloved flower shop. But Fleur had always been more inclined to act on impulse than to think everything out at length. It had got her into lots of trouble at school, notably the time she had rescued a stray mongrel puppy from the canal and taken the dripping mite into the classroom. She glanced at the set, angry face of the man sitting opposite. Nobody could compare *him* to a stray mongrel, but she wished he hadn't shown her that letter from his father. The letter was so simple and affectionate and—perhaps because she was feeling emotional about her own mother—had touched her deeply.

'That's point one dealt with,' he said crisply. 'What's the next?'

He was almost enjoying this now, wasn't he? The organisation, the planning, the dealing with obstacles. This was the other part of his life—the part that didn't contain Melissa and wasn't affected by her desertion. Men seemed to be good at doing that, at living their lives in separate compartments.

'Well, there's my mother's shop,' she said. 'I don't want to close it down, and I have stock already ordered.'

'Haven't you an assistant?'

'Only a young girl—the one who rang up just now. She's a nice girl, but not particularly reliable and certainly not experienced enough to take over.'

'Ye-es.' He fixed his eyes on the ceiling. The great brain working, Fleur thought cynically; the captain of industry! If she could laugh at him, even to herself, it might help to dispel this stupid self-consciousness she felt when he came near her.

He lowered his head. 'Got it!' he said triumphantly. 'This is where my secretary can help out. Mrs Black is what is known as the perfect secretary. I've never found a challenge that she can't handle. We'll get in touch with her as soon as we get to London, and she can travel down on the night train tomorrow and be ready to take over the shop on Monday morning. She's a keen gardener and I'm willing to bet she's familiar with all or any of the flowers you could confront her with. Anyone else at this end who could help?'

'Well, there's Caroline Dunn,' Fleur said doubtfully. 'She has the jewellery shop across the passage and we sometimes take over for each other when we need to go out to see customers or anything like that.'

'Excellent. Can you get in touch with her? Now?'

He was really getting into top gear; he took her breath away. 'I suppose so. But what on earth do I tell her?'

He waved a casual hand. 'Tell her you've been called away suddenly to visit a sick relative. That's near enough to the truth.'

Fleur's lips twisted. 'You don't mind bending the truth to suit your own ends, do you, Mr Stevens? All right, I'll see if I can get her on the phone at home.'

Caroline answered the phone herself. She sounded a little hazy, and Fleur guessed that she and her Johnny were passing a pleasant Saturday afternoon in Caroline's flat. 'Oh, yes, sure,' she said, when Fleur had made her request. 'I'll do anything I can, love. Tell this Mrs Black to call in and see me when she gets here—give her my address—and then we can work something out.' She yawned. 'I hope this relative of yours in France gets better—an aunt, is it?'

'That's right, and thanks a lot, pal,' Fleur said, feeling guilty. Lying didn't come easily to her. She replaced the phone on its stand, with a passing picture of Caroline turning back lazily into Johnny's arms. For some reason she found the picture faintly disturbing.

'OK?' Eliot questioned, and she nodded. 'Good. And the next query?'

'What about my mother? I can't go away and leave the shop in someone else's care without any explanation. What if she phones and finds Mrs Black in charge? She'd be worried to death.'

'Yes,' he said. He thought for a moment, then he shot the question at her. 'How long is she staying in the US?'

Fleur glared at him. 'You should have been a barrister, Mr Stevens. With your technique, you'd have the witnesses groggy in no time at all.'

'I'm going to take that as a compliment,' he said. 'And couldn't you start calling me Eliot?'

'Very well,' she said, 'Eliot.' It was surprising how difficult it was to get his name out. Three years at university had ironed out any shyness she had started with at eighteen, but she had never met a man in Eliot Stevens's league before. 'And my mother plans to stay on for another week or so.'

He nodded thoughtfully. 'It's tricky, isn't it? If you phoned it wouldn't be easy to enter into long explanations, and the story might seem very far-fetched. I would suggest that you write to her now and tell her exactly what has happened. Is it likely that she might phone you here or at the shop?'

Fleur had to admit that it was very unlikely. Her mother didn't belong to the modern high-tech world that took international phone calls for granted.

'Well, we'll brief Mrs Black about what to say, just in case. We don't want your mother to be worried. Any more questions?'

'Clothes,' said Fleur. 'I can't go on any sort of honeymoon, even a phoney one, without thinking about what I'm going to wear—and my life-style certainly doesn't match up to yours,' she added practically, with a glance at the expensively tailored morning-suit he was wearing.

'No problem,' Eliot said crisply. He wasn't going to enter into a discussion of life-styles, that was for sure, and Fleur found herself resenting once more his calm assumption of superiority. 'Just pack a nightie and a toothbrush, and we'll fit you out before we leave London. OK?'

'OK.' Fleur sighed.

He glanced at her quickly. 'Not having second thoughts, are you? Because——'

She pulled a rueful face. 'I've already had second thoughts—and third—and fourth. But don't worry, I won't back out now, I won't let you down. Oh!' She put a hand to her mouth. 'I'm sorry, that was tactless—I didn't mean it that way,' she gasped as she saw his face suddenly go stony and knew that he had crossed the border back into that other compartment of his life, where his lost love and the humiliating let-down at the church waited to torture him.

He looked at her as if he wasn't seeing her. 'You'd better get on with writing that letter,' he said.

Fleur walked over to her mother's small writing-desk. She must be careful what she said to the man; she wouldn't want to rub salt into the wound. What sort of girl, she wondered as she got out writing-pad and biro, would behave as Melissa had behaved? Hadn't she loved him at all? The memory came back to Fleur of that look on the girl's face—she had thought it was fear. That was strange and inexplicable too, because although Eliot Stevens could be masterful and intimidating—she had experienced that herself when she'd accosted him in the passage by the quay—somehow he didn't seem to her the kind of man to strike terror into a girl he had asked to marry him.

She picked up the biro and wrote, 'Darling Mum——' and then stopped and sighed. She would certainly find out more about Eliot Stevens in the next few days, but there was no doubt in her mind that she herself was a hundred per cent tougher than the fragile Melissa, and that it would take more than Eliot Stevens to inspire fear in *her*.

The beginning of the letter took a long time to write, and it wasn't easy. She was uncomfortably conscious of Eliot Stevens's long body, sunk broodingly into the arm-chair behind her as she wrote, and the more she tried to put the words in a way that would not send Janet into a turmoil of anxiety, the more complicated and round-about her sentences became. Finally, disgusted with her own efforts, she crushed up the page and tossed it into the waste-basket.

'Having trouble?' Eliot's voice came mildly from behind her.

She spun round on him. 'Of course I'm having trouble,' she snapped. 'I've got to convince my mother that I haven't taken complete leave of my senses, and it isn't easy.'

'Why not write it down exactly as it happened,' he suggested, 'and let me put in a word or two at the end?'

'What good would that do?' she retorted, exasperated. 'She doesn't know you.'

'She will certainly know me in the future, so we may as well get acquainted now, if it's only by letter. Go on, Fleur,' he encouraged her. 'Just the facts, that's all you need.'

'Oh, all right.' She swung back to the desk, took out a fresh sheet, and began again. 'Darling Mum, You're not going to believe it, but this is what happened yesterday——'

When she thought of it as putting down the unembroidered facts, it wasn't so difficult, but when she got to the end it got more tricky. Eventually she wrote, 'So, you see, I felt that I couldn't refuse. Please understand and don't worry about me. I get a strong feeling that I'm doing the right thing in everyone's interests, and I just couldn't bear to think of the shop having to close. Eliot insists on adding a note to this letter, so I'll say goodbye now and phone you when you've had the chance to read this. Your letter arrived yesterday and I'm so very, very glad you're feeling better. There are good times ahead, I'm sure. Lots and lots of love, and love to Aunt Brenda, Your Fleur.'

'There you are,' she said resignedly. 'You can add your bit if you must.'

'I must.' He was on his feet behind her chair. Not giving her a chance to get up, he leaned over her shoulder. 'May I borrow your pen? I don't carry mine around in this outfit.'

Their hands brushed as he took the pen from her fingers, and again there was that electric current passing between them that left Fleur's whole arm feeling weak. It must, however, be a one-way current, she decided, for he certainly didn't seem aware of it. She watched as he scribbled in a bold, confident hand, 'You have the nicest, kindest daughter and I promise you faithfully to take good care of her. I look forward to our meeting very soon. Yours gratefully, Eliot Stevens.'

'There,' he said. 'Now you address the envelope and give it to me, and we'll send it off Swiftair as soon as we find a post office open. With any luck your mother should get the letter on Tuesday, so you can phone her Tuesday evening and set any of her doubts at rest. That OK with you?'

'I suppose so,' Fleur said with a shrug of resignation. She wasn't accustomed to being organised at this speed, but of course Eliot was a businessman and it was all second nature to him. She sealed the letter and gave it to him, wondering how she had come to put her trust in this man so quickly and so completely. She only hoped she wasn't making an utter fool of herself.

He groped irritably inside the black morning-coat for a pocket. 'Lord, I wish I could get out of this fancy dress. I shan't feel like a human being until I'm wearing something normal again.' He ran a finger round inside his collar. 'Mind if I discard the neck decoration?' He pulled off the grey silk cravat and tossed it on to a chair. The black coat followed, together with the stiff white collar. 'That's better,' he sighed in relief, unbuttoning the top buttons of his shirt.

He glanced at Fleur's somewhat alarmed face. 'Don't worry,' he said, 'the disrobing will go no further.' His mouth twisted bitterly as he added, 'I quite realise that a marriage has *not* taken place.'

Fleur stifled a gasp. This wasn't the same man who had buried his face in his hands such a short time ago and muttered brokenly, 'I love her, you know. I'm crazy about the little fool.'

'Please——' she murmured inadequately, not quite knowing what she was pleading for. Perhaps for him to show more of the pain that was inside him, not to bottle up his feelings. 'I'm so—so sorry——'

He must have read her thoughts, for he turned on her savagely. 'Pack it in, for God's sake, girl. You mustn't expect me to weep crocodile tears over my sad plight. I don't expect tea and sympathy. What's happened is past. We learn from it if we're wise, and then go on to the future.' Almost as an afterthought, he added, 'I shall just be very careful not to make the same mistake again, that's all.' He drew in a harsh breath, then said quite evenly, 'Now then, how are we going to fill in the time until it gets dark and we can leave? Suppose you show me round your garden for a start? It looks interesting.'

And that, thought Fleur, summed up the situation and set the tone for the days ahead. He didn't want her understanding and he certainly didn't want her pity. He would keep her at arm's length, that was the message. Which was the best thing that could happen, wasn't it?

So it was strange that, as she led the way out to the garden, she should feel so curiously disappointed.

CHAPTER FOUR

IT WASN'T until the following morning, as the taxi that had brought them from Paddington station was trundling along the empty Sunday morning London streets, that the alarming reality of what she was doing hit Fleur like a blow in the stomach.

She'd been flying high ever since she agreed to Eliot's plan yesterday. What she had promised to do was nothing very much, after all, she had assured herself. And the wonderful, wonderful thing was that she would save the flower shop for Janet. Something that she had set her heart on doing. Something that she could never have hoped to accomplish with so little effort in any other way.

She had almost enjoyed the thrill of the creepy cloak and dagger episode of driving the van, in darkness, to the deserted church, leaving it there and picking up Eliot's hired car, where they found his travelling bag still safe and sound in the boot. She had definitely enjoyed the unheard-of luxury of the first-class single sleeper on the night train, the novelty of being wakened with morning tea when the train was stationary in the echoing gloom of London's Paddington station at six-thirty on Sunday morning.

But now, as the taxi turned into the King's Road, the full implication of what was ahead became clear. This was Eliot Stevens's world she was entering—a world of affluence and Top People, a world where all the women looked like something out of *Vogue* and all the rooms in the houses came straight from *Ideal Home*; where bored rich people drifted from Henley Regatta to Ascot Races; from dinner at the Savoy to a box at the opera, and—Fleur's imagination boggled.

Somehow she had to keep her end up in the midst of all this, but she wasn't going to pretend she was accustomed to luxury and high living. Eliot would just have to take her as she was.

'Where are we going?' she enquired, glancing up at the dark, abstracted face of the man sitting beside her. He had talked very little since they'd left the cottage. That was understandable; he had a lot to think about. But Fleur was by nature a communicator, and she found the long silences somewhat unnerving.

'Chelsea,' he said. 'An old house overlooking the river. We bought it—or rather, my father did—many years ago, before prices went through the roof in those parts. It was when he was starting up the company and was one of the first renovation jobs they did.'

He was talking about something that interested him at last! Perhaps she could encourage him to open up a bit.

'Is that what your company specialises in? Renovation work?' she asked.

He nodded, and she saw a flicker of amusement in the dark blue eyes. 'Exactly. Did you think all we did was pull down beautiful old buildings and put modern monstrosities in their place?'

Fleur felt her cheeks go warm. 'That's what I did think at first,' she admitted. 'I was worried about the flower shop and I feared the worst.'

'Hm, well, that proves that you shouldn't jump to conclusions, doesn't it?'

'Are you lecturing me?' Fleur glared at him. She hadn't *had* to admit to her mistake; it was odious of him to put her down like that. This was the Eliot Stevens she had first encountered in the quayside passage, the disdainful, aloof man she had disliked on sight.

'No, merely stating an obvious truth,' he said blandly.

Fleur stared out of the window as the taxi trundled along the King's Road. Beast! Horrid, superior beast! And she had to pretend to be madly in love with him. It wasn't going to be easy.

The taxi turned down a short side road, rounded a corner on to Chelsea Embankment and pulled up outside an enormous house, higher and wider than the ones on either side of it, with a flight of stone steps leading up to a massive front door whose brass fittings gleamed in the early morning sunlight. There were narrow wrought-iron balconies all along the first floor, and a garage beneath the level of the ground floor.

'Lovely old house,' Eliot mused as he put his key in the lock. 'It was a pity to carve it up, but it would take a Victorian-size family to fill it and a fleet of servants to look after it. My place is on the first floor—come on, we'll walk up, it's not worth taking the lift.'

He led the way to an elegantly curving staircase that rose from a lofty hall. Floor and stairs were close-carpeted in muted grey. Brass urns containing tall, spreading plants with glossy leaves were placed in strategic corners. The plants were unfamiliar to Fleur and she would have liked to stop and have a closer look at them, but Eliot was taking the shallow stairs two at a time and she hurried after him.

He unlocked a white door on the first landing and stood aside to usher her in. Inside there were more white doors leading off an octagonal entrance hall. Eliot threw them open one by one. 'Bedroom. Shower-room. Kitchen. Living-room. Very compact, as you can see. As an honoured guest you can have the bedroom, and I'll kip down on the sofa in here.'

Fleur followed him into the living-room and stared around her, wide-eyed. A prestige room in a prestige apartment! Long and high, furnished in a modern—but not aggressively modern—style. A masculine room, with pale squashy leather furniture, low tables of smoky glass, built-in cupboards, shelves with flowering plants, books, a compact stereo unit. Double, floor-length windows with cinnamon velvet curtains opened on to a wrought-iron balcony. And the view! Across the Embankment to the River Thames and beyond the slate-grey water to Battersea on the South Bank, hazy in the faint morning mist. Fleur tried to imagine what it would cost to run an apartment like this—what kind of life-style it represented—what his friends would be like. She was way out of her depth here; she wouldn't be able to hold her own, or convince anyone, in the part she had agreed to play.

Eliot dumped his bag against the wall and strode across to throw open both the long windows, letting in a cool breeze off the river. 'Nice to get a spot of fresh air before the traffic gets going,' he remarked conversationally. 'We have to shut the windows then, and turn on the air-conditioner. Going to be a hot day. Now, let's go and see what we can rustle up for breakfast and then I'll do some phoning.'

He grinned encouragingly at Fleur, who was standing in the middle of the room.

'What's the matter, Fleur?' he said, on a faint note of irritation.

She turned her back on him. 'I feel like a spare part,' she muttered crossly. 'I don't know what I'm supposed to be doing.' She whirled round to face him. 'This flat—I've only seen flats like this on the telly. It's no use pretending I'm at home in a place like this. It makes me feel like Little Orphan Annie. And I'm supposed to be feeling like your wife. I don't think I can do it.'

'Rubbish,' he said briskly. 'You're a very pretty girl——' His gaze passed assessingly over her, lingered on the long, silken legs, moved slowly up over the parts that were hidden by her straight white jacket, and came to rest on her face, a lively, small face with flawless skin and wide, green eyes that were meeting his own uncertainly. 'Very pretty indeed,' he repeated. He touched the bright curls that framed her face. 'I suppose I wouldn't be saying anything very original if I told you that your hair is the colour of ripe chestnuts? Lots of men must have told you that.'

He paused, and when she didn't answer he moved closer. 'And as for feeling like my wife,' he said softly, 'how about a little practice?'

It was so sudden, so completely unexpected, that Fleur hadn't time to resist when his arms went round her and his mouth came down on hers. His lips were cool and

firm against her own with a pressure that was—was—
in the midst of her surprise her mind searched for a
word—sexless, was the only one that seemed to fit. Resentment flared. He was going to work on her as if she
were a raw young actress and he the lordly director,
deigning to stoop from his great height to throw her a
crumb of comfort, a word of encouragement. It was a—
a *patronising* kiss, an insulting kiss. He drew away
looking down into her face, obviously pleased with
himself. 'There,' he said, smiling, 'did that help?'

It was the culmination of everything the last twenty-
four hours had been leading up to. But the strength of
the fury that gripped Fleur was unexpected. She had
never been so angry in her life before, boiling, seething
with it, wanting to lacerate the smiling face that looked
down so complacently into hers. How dared he? How
dared he? Her anger reached for any verbal weapon that
would hurt him, take that hateful condescending smile
off his face.

Her lip curled. 'No, it didn't. If that's the best you
can do, Mr Eliot Stevens, I can understand why your
bride walked out on you.'

He stiffened, going very still. His eyes narrowed
dangerously, the colour drained from his face. For a
second Fleur thought he was going to strike her, and she
recoiled, suddenly ashamed at what she had said.

'You bitch. You damned little bitch! I'd like to bloody
well——'

Fleur never heard what he would like to do. What he
actually did do was to grab hold of her and pull her
roughly against him, so roughly that she felt as if her
ribs were cracking. Her mouth opened to protest, but

before she could utter a word his own mouth had covered it savagely, hurtfully, his fingers digging into her arms as he held her in a grip that was brutal in its strength. There was nothing patronising about this kiss. It was the unleashing of masculine violence that was terrifying in its intensity, an assault of his mouth on hers that went on and on until she was fighting for breath—until somewhere deep inside she was aware of an equally passionate response stirring, a shocking need to claw, to bite. She twisted her head from side to side unavailingly. His mouth still ravaged hers, his hands still steel-strong on her arms.

Then, suddenly, it was over. He pushed her away and she fell back on to the leather sofa, gasping for breath, spasmodic shudders passing through her. She groped in her coat pocket for a handkerchief and pressed it to her aching mouth.

Fleur hadn't been conscious of Eliot going out of the room, but now he was nowhere to be seen. She wondered how soon she could get back to Cornwall. Because of course she couldn't stay here, she couldn't possibly continue with Eliot Stevens's plan, not after what had just happened. With shaking hands she opened her handbag and counted the cash inside. Seven pounds and some loose change. Not nearly enough to pay her fare; she didn't even own a student railcard now. She tried to remember if any of the girls in her year at college lived in London, but she didn't think any of them did. Anyway, she hadn't had any bosom friends on whom she could suddenly descend with a request for a loan. She would have to ask Eliot for money. Surely he would see that she wouldn't be prepared to go on with his plan after what had happened? *Surely* he would? But she didn't know anything *surely* about Eliot Stevens. She didn't know anything at all about him.

The smell of coffee drifted into the room, and she looked round to see Eliot coming in with a tray. He placed it on a low table beside the sofa and sank into a deep chair opposite.

'This will revive us for starters,' he said, 'then we can go into the kitchen and make toast—if that's what you'd like.'

Just like that! A smile, an ordinary tone of voice! As if nothing unusual had happened a few minutes ago. As if he hadn't—hadn't—attacked her like a wild beast!

'Black? White? In between?' He held the coffee-pot aloft.

'Black,' muttered Fleur, and he poured a cup out and pushed it towards her across the table.

She took a gulp and put the cup down. 'I'd like to leave as soon as possible, please. I'll have to ask you for my fare home; I haven't enough cash on me at present.'

'Leave?' The dark brows rose, the wide forehead creased. 'Why?'

'Why?' She stared at him in disbelief. 'You ask me why? I'd have thought it was obvious.'

He shook his head, puzzled. 'Not to me it isn't.' Then light appeared to dawn. 'Not because I kissed you? Surely you haven't taken offence at a small thing like a kiss?'

The man was incredible. He looked genuinely surprised. 'You may have thought it a small thing,' Fleur said. 'To me it appeared to be a vicious attack.' She dabbed at her swollen lip.

'Oh, dear,' Eliot said. 'Did I do that? I'm sorry, Fleur. But you did provoke me, you know. Surely you realise that you can't make a remark like that to a man and get away with it?'

He was being so *reasonable*, the beast. And she did feel faintly guilty about what she had said on the spur of the moment.

'Yes, I suppose so,' she mumbled. 'I'm sorry I said what I did.'

'And I'm sorry if I upset you,' Eliot replied quickly. 'And now that's cleared up, suppose we go and have some breakfast?' He held out a hand in the friendliest manner to pull her up from the depths of the sofa. Damn him, he'd got his own way again, Fleur thought, pointedly ignoring the hand he held out to her.

The kitchen was very modern, as might have been expected, and fitted with all the expensive gadgets that Fleur's mother had always coveted but had never been able to afford. The units had pale sycamore doors and pure white tops and there was a spacious breakfast-bar at one end of the room. Eliot had set it with tomato-red plates, jars of honey and marmalade and butter, and there was an appetising smell of toasting bread issuing from the toaster.

'Sit yourself down.' He pulled out a high stool and went back to the living-room for the coffee-tray. He was being very much the pleasant host now. All for a purpose of course, Fleur recognised. He was manipulating her delicately, as a fisherman would play a wily fish until he had it hooked well and truly on the end of his line. But she wouldn't be fooled. She knew now what he was like under the pleasant, reasonable front he chose to put on.

A few minutes ago she had provoked him into showing her his real self, the dark, violent man who had frightened her with his brutal handling of her—frightened her, yet—yet—— Once again she felt inside her the uncomfortable stirring of a passion she had never experienced before.

Before they had finished breakfast, a buzzer sounded in the hall. Eliot went to answer it and in a few moments returned, followed by a thick-set, youngish man with corn-gold hair. Fleur recognised the colour of that hair—she couldn't be mistaken, even though she had only seen it from the back. Eliot's best man.

He was talking as they came into the kitchen. '—thought you might have made it back home, so I called in early on spec, and——'

Brown eyes opened wide as he saw Fleur sitting at the breakfast-bar. The square, good-natured face expressed volumes, which Fleur didn't particularly want to read. She could hazard a guess at what he was thinking.

Eliot had picked up the message, too. He smiled crookedly. 'Fleur, meet Toby Armstrong, my architect and my very good friend. Toby, this is Fleur Gold, whose presence here will be explained in due course. And it's not what you might think, pal,' he added pointedly. 'Coffee, Toby?' Eliot filled a mug from the coffee-pot, which seemed to be inexhaustible, and pulled out another stool.

'First,' he said, 'put me in the picture as to what happened after I made my escape yesterday.'

There was an awkward little silence as Toby glanced uncomfortably towards Fleur.

'Oh, don't worry, old chap,' Eliot added hastily. 'Fleur's been in this from the start. As a matter of fact, she did the flowers in the church and made the bride's bouquet—which didn't figure in the proceedings,' he added with a twist of his lips.

'I see,' Toby said, and it was plain that he didn't. But he took a gulp of his coffee and said, 'Well, most of us drifted along to the Templetons' house and partook of lunch in a marquee, and at first it had all the hilarity of a funeral wake. But after the serving wenches brought on the champagne things began to loosen up a bit, and in the end people were fraternising. You know how it is—anything in the nature of a disaster draws folk together. There was, naturally, a good deal of speculation going on as to exactly what had happened, and the only person to hazard an informed guess was a fellow who turned out to be a great-uncle of your——' he glanced apologetically at Eliot '—of Melissa's. On her father's side. An old army type. "Never thought she'd go through with it," he barked. "Wasn't surprising she went AWOL."' Toby glanced at Fleur and added, 'You know, Absent Without Leave.'

Eliot's face was a set mask. 'Well?' he rapped out. 'Did he say why?'

Toby shook his head dolefully. 'Only said, "Look at that mother of hers—girl never had a chance."' The fair man rubbed his chin in an awkward way. 'Damned bad luck, old boy. I'm sorry.'

Eliot nodded absently. 'Well, it's over and done with now and best forgotten. I'm going to put the whole blasted mess behind me.'

'Good!' Toby cheered up immediately. 'Very best thing you could do. Spilt milk and all that!'

Eliot ignored that. He slid off his high stool. 'Be back in a few minutes,' he said, not looking at either of the other two. 'Phone call I've just remembered.' And he walked quickly out of the kitchen.

Toby blew out his cheeks and expelled a gust of air. He glanced at Fleur, who hadn't moved during the conversation and had kept her eyes on her plate. 'Cut up, isn't he, poor old lad?' he muttered. 'I'd say it was a lucky break, though. He'd have been crawling up the walls with boredom after a few weeks of having that Melissa chick for a wife.'

Fleur felt she had to say something. 'He was in love with her—he said so. He was devastated when she let him down.'

Toby gave her an old-fashioned look. 'Oh, yeah? Love? What's that? You tell me.'

He had a comical, clown's face. A big mouth and large, mournful brown eyes under the yellow thatch of hair. An extrovert, Fleur thought; you couldn't not like him and he would be impossible to squash.

'Oh, you're a cynic,' she said and she started to gather together the breakfast plates and stack them in the sink. 'It's no good explaining to you.'

The buzzer sounded again. 'That'll be my lady-love,' Toby grinned. 'Mandy promised to come on here to meet me when she managed to get the sleep out of her eyes.' He wandered off into the hall.

Fleur sat down and waited. She was certainly being thrown in at the deep end—meeting Eliot's friends at the earliest possible moment. But if they were none of them more alarming than Toby she had nothing to worry about. She smiled as she realised that she had been picturing them as a snooty, trendy set who would shake her self-confidence—as Eliot had done.

'Fleur——' Eliot called from the living-room. 'Come here a minute.'

She felt resentment rise and almost she ignored his command. She wasn't a child, to be summoned like that. But she swallowed her pride and made her way across the hall and into the living-room.

Mandy was draped across the sofa. Straight, black, glossy hair, huge black eyes, near-black skin, wearing a sleeveless white silk dress and rows and rows of orange-coloured beads. West Indian? Asian? Whatever she was, she was absolutely gorgeous, Fleur thought, going across to hold out her hand as Toby sketched an introduction.

'Hello, Fleur.' A beautiful, husky voice. A dazzling white smile. 'Come and sit by me.' She patted the sofa. If she was surprised to see Fleur instead of the absent Melissa, she wasn't showing it.

Eliot went out and came back with another mug of coffee from the widow's cruse of a coffee-pot. 'Drink up, Mandy,' he instructed, perching on the arm of the sofa. 'We're going to need your assistance.'

Mandy flashed him a smile, full of warmth and sympathy, reaching up to touch his arm with a satiny dark hand gleaming with gold rings. 'Anything I can do, darling. Too bad about the wedding—Toby told me. I'm sorry.'

'Thanks, Mandy, that's all finished and forgotten,' Eliot said shortly. For a moment his mouth set grimly. Then he looked at Toby. 'But it left me in a jam—I told

you about my dad—and I was worried stiff about how
he would take it when I turned up without the new wife
he's been expecting and looking forward to. He's been
pretty low lately, and the last thing I wanted was to go
and weep on his shoulder—metaphorically speaking,' he
added with a faint grin.

'Fortunately,' he went on, 'I had a bright idea.'

'Trust you,' Toby put in. 'Ideas man, our Eliot.'

Eliot ignored that. 'I won't go into details, but the
outcome is that Fleur here has been very helpful and
agreed to fill the vacancy.'

Mandy clapped her hands. 'You mean——' The lus-
trous dark eyes turned from Eliot to Fleur and back
again. 'You are going to marry? That's wonderful.'

Eliot put on a wry expression. 'Well, not exactly,
Mandy. It's going to be more in the nature of a business
arrangement. I'm going to take Fleur to visit my dad—
as my wife. I'm sure we can carry it off, and it will make
him so happy. Fleur stands to benefit from our arrangement, too,' he added. 'Don't you, Fleur?'

Fleur had been watching Eliot while this had been
going on. She was beginning to get the feel of his moods
now. If she was going to pretend to be married to him
she would have to work at getting to know as much as
she could about him. About the real Eliot Stevens. So
far she knew that he had a quick temper that flared up
but that died out just as quickly. That he could be arrogant and dismissive, but that he probably didn't realise that he was being hurtful to other people. That he
could be loyal and affectionate. And—above all—that
he had an intensely passionate nature. She had seen it

when he had looked at Melissa. And she had experienced it when he had kissed her a few minutes ago.

Armed with this knowledge, she decided that the best way to deal with him was to be cool and co-operative and forget about the resentment that still smouldered inside. That wouldn't get her anywhere. The one thing she wouldn't do was allow him to walk over her or to patronise her.

'Well, of course,' she said composedly, having reached this conclusion in a split second—which was the way Fleur usually reached conclusions. 'It works both ways. Otherwise Eliot would hardly have expected me to agree, I'm sure.' She smiled at Mandy and at Toby, who was lolling over the back of the sofa, stroking Mandy's smooth neck. 'But I hasten to add that the benefit was not financial reward, was it, Eliot?' She raised neatly marked eyebrows in his direction.

He met her gaze and held it, and a little frisson of tension spiralled through her. She had surprised him and she was delighted. Now, she thought, they could meet on equal terms. For the first time she wasn't slightly in awe of him. He would no longer think of her as 'the little flower-girl'.

'Certainly not,' he said. 'Not in pounds and pence. But Fleur will need a trousseau——' he looked towards Mandy '—and she has agreed to allow me to supply that. You see, she didn't expect to be going away on a honeymoon quite so soon, did you, my sweet?' The glance he slid towards Fleur was faintly mocking. Honours even, she thought.

'So this is where you come in, Mandy. Will you take her along later on today and buy her all she will need for a week down at San Remo, and send me the bill? You can open your boutique on a Sunday, just to oblige a friend?'

Mandy bounced with pleasure on the sofa. 'Of course I can, and that will be lovely—and so good for business.' She threw a wicked glance upwards at Toby. 'You see, my darling, I shall be able to declare a profit, after all.'

'Mandy runs a boutique in Kensington,' Eliot explained to Fleur.

And Toby added, with a ruefully comic smile, 'And if it starts to pay she'll get big-headed, so don't spend too much, Fleur.'

Mandy threw him a nasty look. 'We shall ignore the cost,' she told him, 'and Fleur will have the most beautiful trousseau and she will look like a million dollars.' She reached out and touched Fleur's silky mop of curls. 'Exquisite,' she crooned. 'And what a figure! Oh, I'm going to enjoy dressing you, Fleur.'

Toby grinned. 'The difference between the sexes,' he murmured.

Mandy twisted her neck to look up at him. 'What are you saying?'

'Only that a man would enjoy *un*dressing Fleur,' he told her wickedly.

'Oh—you,' Mandy pouted. She got to her feet. 'I shall take this man away before he disgraces me further. We're going down to the coast to visit Toby's aunt,' she explained. 'Will you bring Fleur to the boutique this afternoon, about five, Eliot?'

It was arranged, and Toby and Mandy left in high spirits, running down the stairs teasing each other.

'I liked them,' Fleur said rather wistfully. The two of them had brought a breath of fresh air into the rather down-beat atmosphere.

'They're good friends,' Eliot said. 'They're the only people we need to tell about our little ploy—with the exception of Mrs Black, of course. I'll ring her at home now and get her to come round here as soon as she can.' He went into the bedroom to phone.

Mrs Black—the perfect secretary! Another hurdle to cross, Fleur thought with a sinking heart. She couldn't imagine that even a perfect secretary would be able to take her place at Porthgurran Flowers and keep the shop ticking over satisfactorily. Somehow Fleur imagined her as young and snooty and highly trained. And, if so, she wouldn't get on at all well with the scatterbrained Betty.

But again she was in for a surprise. Mrs Black arrived within half an hour and turned out to be a plumpish woman in her middle forties with large gold-rimmed glasses and rather untidy fair hair.

She was certainly the perfect unflappable secretary. Eliot had evidently sketched in the position when he spoke to her on the phone, and she greeted Fleur with calm and impersonal politeness, brought out notebook and biro, and sat expectantly waiting for directions.

When Eliot had briefed her she raised her neat head and read back her shorthand notes.

'I travel on the night train from Paddington. On arrival pick up a hire car, a black Rover, Number E423 FKT—drive to Porthgurran, take up residence at Penrath Cottage, then contact a Miss Caroline Dunn at the address given, who will take me to the florist's shop and put me in the picture there as far as possible. Later I find the shop van at the local church.' She looked up at Eliot. 'Does this Miss Dunn know the details of your—er—plan?'

'No, and she mustn't. The fewer people who know, the better,' he said quickly. 'She only knows that Fleur has had to go abroad to visit a sick relative. Toby and Mandy and you yourself are the only ones who know the whole story. Oh, and we've written to Fleur's mother, in the US on holiday. If by some stroke of bad luck she should phone before she has received the letter, please reassure her that Fleur has had to go away for a day or two and that she will be getting a letter of explanation immediately. I think that's the lot. Can you cope, do you think, Joan? Yes, I'm sure you can.'

'I shall enjoy a week in Cornwall,' Mrs Black assured him calmly. 'And I'll do my best to keep the shop running smoothly. I love flowers,' she added to Fleur, as if to reassure her. 'And now, if I may have the keys?'

Fleur groped in her handbag and Eliot disappeared into the bedroom to find the car keys.

Mrs Black looked after him and the cultivated calm had gone from her face. Her pale cheeks were suddenly pink with anger. 'What a beastly shame!' she exclaimed hotly. 'He's such a *wonderful* person—what girl could let him down like that? And he was so devoted to her, you could tell!'

'Yes,' said Fleur. She was getting a little tired of contemplating Eliot's devotion to Melissa Templeton.

'You must look after him,' the secretary went on earnestly. 'See he gets enough to eat and make him rest. He's been overdoing it ever since he got engaged—missing his sleep.'

Fleur almost giggled. 'I'll make sure he doesn't miss his sleep,' she said gravely, and Mrs Black shot her a suspicious look, but at that moment Eliot returned with the car keys, and the studiedly placid expression returned. Fleur added the keys of the van, the shop and the cottage, and, as Mrs Black tucked them all away in her capacious brown handbag, had a brief moment of panic, which she quickly subdued. She was in this up to her eyebrows now, she couldn't get out of it.

When the secretary had departed, Eliot sank on to the sofa with a long sigh. 'Well, that's that, all the preliminary work done! What did you think of our Mrs Black—rather marvellous, don't you agree?'

'Oh, yes, she's the perfect secretary, as you said. Even to the point of idolising her boss,' she added with a grin.

'Rubbish!' he said, and she was amused to see him look faintly embarrassed.

'She warned me that you'd been working too hard and said I was to see that you got enough to eat—and enough sleep.' She slipped him a sideways look. 'I hope she didn't get any wrong ideas.'

'Just so long as *you* don't,' he said easily. He patted the place beside him. 'Come and sit down by me, Fleur. We've got a little while to ourselves to get to know each other.'

She remained standing. Eliot was smiling up at her and it was a new kind of smile, a charming smile, which—Eliot being Eliot—couldn't help being devastatingly sexy.

'I think I'll sit here, thanks.' Fleur sat in a chair, some distance away from him.

He raised dark brows expressively. 'Don't hold that kiss against me, I promise not to repeat the performance. I wasn't very proud of myself, but you must admit you asked for it. And as it turned out you did me a good turn.'

'How?' asked Fleur cautiously.

'I'm not quite sure. I think it got something out of my system. I'd been feeling like dirt ever since Melissa left me standing in that church, and it doesn't suit me to feel like dirt. Taking it out on you seemed to—restore my masculine ego to some extent. Do you mind very much?'

A small smile touched Fleur's soft mouth. 'I suppose I can bear it. So long as your ego doesn't need polishing up too often.'

He laughed. 'Do you know, Fleur, I think we're going to hit it off very well. As I said to your mother in the letter, you're a nice girl, and they don't come along too frequently.'

'*Nice!*' She pulled a face.

'I meant it as a compliment,' he said quietly. 'I think by "nice" what I mean is "genuine". You're genuine. And you have warmth too, and I think I discern a sense of humour lurking behind the sparkle in those green eyes.'

He was looking closely into the same green eyes as he spoke, and Fleur's heart began an uneven pattering. 'That's a good build-up.' She smiled brilliantly. 'If I need a PR man, I'll call on you.'

He leaned back in the corner of the sofa, stretching out his long legs in their close-fitting black trousers. He was still wearing the T-shirt he had changed into on the train last night, and its whiteness contrasted with the sun-tanned skin of his neck. Absurdly long black lashes curved over brilliant, sapphire-blue eyes; Fleur swallowed and looked away.

She thought she had recognised and accepted the risks in the scheme she had agreed to. But now she had to admit a risk she hadn't reckoned on—and that risk was sitting right opposite her. He was more attractive than any man had a right to be, and now that he was looking lazily relaxed his attraction had taken on a dangerous, sexy quality.

'I'll be happy to oblige. Now, come and sit beside me, Fleur. I can't talk to you from this distance. We must get used to the idea that we're a newly married couple. Come on, I'm not going to eat you.' He patted the sofa again.

It would have seemed priggish to refuse. She tried to make a joke of it. 'So long as I have your promise of that——' she murmured in mock warning. She got up and joined him on the sofa—at the opposite end.

'That's not where a new wife would sit.' He reached sideways and yanked her towards him. 'You really must use your imagination, my girl.'

That's the trouble—I *am*, Fleur thought. She wished she didn't feel so painfully shy. He put a friendly arm round her shoulders and drew her close and she felt herself stiffen.

He sighed. 'Relax, Fleur, *relax*. It's all part of the game. OK, I know it isn't easy for you. You're wishing it was your Roger sitting here with you and you can't bear the thought of putting me where he should be—right?'

Fleur swallowed. She hadn't thought of Roger for quite some time. She nodded wordlessly.

His arm tightened round her in the friendliest way. 'Yes, I know only too well. It's hell, losing someone you love. But we've both got to make the best of it. Maybe if you could pretend, just now and again, that I *am* Roger, it might help.'

Was that what *he* was going to do? Pretend she was Melissa? 'No,' she shot out. 'No, I couldn't do that. It would be—be—horrible.'

He drew away from her slightly. 'Forget it, then,' he said stiffly. 'It was only a suggestion. I didn't realise I was so repulsive to you.'

Heavens, why had she put it like that? 'Oh, you're not, you're not.' She was nearly in tears. 'I didn't mean it like that. I m-meant that it would be—be dishonest.'

'Well, that's a relief.' There was a smile in his voice now. 'And—just to set the record straight—am I allowed to have a practice kiss? I seem to have muffed the previous two.'

His face was very close to hers. She was almost painfully aware of the clean, masculine smell of his skin. She kept her eyes wide open by a tremendous effort, because to close them would be to admit to the unwelcome fact that she wanted him to kiss her. From only inches away his own eyes were deep blue as the ocean, the long, glossy lashes lowered. She could see every separate lash, every tiny line at the corners of his eyes, feel the warmth of his breath on her cheek.

Somehow she managed a small, half-reluctant grin. 'If you must,' she murmured, and felt his lips come down on hers.

It wasn't in the least like that first, impersonal kiss, and certainly had none of the brutality of the second. Neither, she guessed, was it intended to be arousing. His mouth stroked hers gently and then found its way up her cheek, along her forehead and came down to close both her eyes with butterfly softness, before returning to her mouth.

Suddenly she heard his quick intake of breath, felt the increased pressure on her lips. A pressure which would—in another moment—force them to open. Her treacherous body was on the very brink of inviting that. A slow, subtle warmth was invading her inside. She wanted to reach her arms up and pull him closer—closer——

With a desperate effort she twisted her head away. 'No,' she muttered.

Immediately he released her, drawing in his breath. 'I mustn't let myself get too enthusiastic, must I?' he said ruefully. 'Maybe we'd better restrict our more intimate caresses for public display in future.'

Her reply was so pat that the words must have been arranging themselves inside her brain. 'A honeymoon inside-out, in fact?' she said.

He grinned appreciatively and the moment of danger had passed. 'That's a marvellous way of putting it. And anyway, it's good to know that we're not exactly averse to each other. It should make everything much easier.'

Should it, indeed? Fleur thought. I wish I could believe that.

CHAPTER FIVE

For the next hour or so Fleur had no cause to complain that Eliot was silent. It seemed that he never stopped asking questions. He drew her out about every detail of her childhood in Birmingham and the flower shop where her mother had worked all those years. Of the schools she had gone to, the sports she played, her taste in books, music, films. Her years at London University, the flat she shared latterly with two other girls.

'And at university you read——?'

'Art history, mostly Northern European.' She sighed impatiently. 'I feel like a specimen under a microscope. You know all there is to know about me now.'

His smile was mocking. 'Not quite all. You notice I've only asked about the things that would naturally interest a man about the girl he was going to marry. I haven't enquired about your love-life.'

Fleur raised her eyebrows. 'You wouldn't be interested in the love-life of the girl you were going to marry, then?'

'Well, what do *you* think? I'm only human—I'd be interested all right. But I wouldn't expect to be told unless the information was volunteered freely. And even then I'm not sure that it would be wise to accept a one-sided confidence.'

'You wouldn't be prepared to return the compliment?'

'What—give a résumé of *my* love-life? No way,' he said firmly. 'As you may have gathered, it's the present and the future I'm concerned with. The past is over and done with.'

She saw the way his eyes seemed to darken and knew he was thinking of Melissa. Who is he trying to fool? she wondered. Me? Himself?

In a businesslike tone she said, 'Well, now you know all about me. What should I know about you if I'm supposed to be your new wife?'

He shrugged, reeling off bare facts. 'Childhood with parents—father and stepmother—at house on the river with big garden. Rather lonely at first—said parents bickering most of the time. A child never really gets used to it.' His face darkened for a moment, then brightened again. 'It was better when I went away to school. The usual schools, then Cambridge to read architecture. A couple of years of knocking around the world on a shoestring. Then into the business with my dad. Travelling about looking for suitable old buildings to work on. I was soon fascinated by the whole thing and have remained so, as you know. I took over the business when my dad retired.'

'No brothers or sisters?'

He shook his head. 'I'm an only. That's something we have in common, Fleur. Only children are supposed to be spoilt, but I'm darned sure you weren't, and I didn't get much spoiling either. My stepmother wasn't the maternal type—she was relieved to get me away to school when I was seven.' His mouth twisted and Fleur felt a pang of regret for a relationship that should have been close and loving and obviously had been very far from that. 'I've always got on well with my dad, but fathers don't often have time to spoil little boys.'

He leaned his head against the back of the sofa. 'So that's all you need to know about me. No doubt you'll pick up a few more odds and ends as we go along.'

'How long have we known each other, and where did we meet?' Fleur enquired, folding her hands in her lap.

He considered that. 'I'm trying to remember what I told my dad about Melissa when I wrote to say we were getting married.' Again he brought out the name with nonchalance. Fleur glanced at him quickly, wondering how much it cost him to do that, but she learned nothing from his face. He might have been speaking of any casual acquaintance rather than the girl he had only yesterday confessed to being crazily in love with. *Could* men forget so quickly and easily? she wondered.

'We met in Cornwall, of course,' he said slowly. 'So that applies to you and me, too.'

'When?' Fleur enquired. 'That seems important.'

He frowned slightly. 'Yes. Well, it all happened very quickly. I was doing some business in London with John Templeton and he invited me to his home in Porthgurran for a weekend visit. That was at the end of June. I first saw Melissa there.' He was looking out of the window at the white feathery clouds as they drifted slowly across the sky, putting a silver sparkle here and there on the river, and his eyes were suddenly unfocused. 'She was standing at the edge of the cliff—and the wind was blowing through her hair and she was wearing——' He broke off. 'What the hell does it matter what she was wearing?' he finished quite violently.

He turned and looked at Fleur apologetically.

'Sorry, Fleur. I don't mean to sound like a love-sick calf. It just gets you now and then. Love's a funny thing—you can't fall either in or out of it to order. It just happens. I expect you find that with your Roger?'

Fleur sighed. 'Yes.' It would be better if he believed that she was pining for Roger. It evened things up a bit. Because he had just answered her unspoken question. He had surely *not* put behind him his love for Melissa.

'But to go back to what we were talking about——' Eliot's voice was businesslike again. 'It's ridiculous, but I can't remember how much I said in my letters to my father. I remember I went on a bit about how lovely Melissa is, but there isn't any problem there.' His eyes passed over Fleur with frank assessment. 'You're lovely too, Fleur.'

'Thank you,' she said rather tartly.

'In a very different way, of course.'

'Of course.'

Roman slave-girls must have felt like this when they were put up for sale. But he hadn't the faintest idea that his words, or the way he spoke them, could possibly be hurtful to her, had he? Consideration for other people's feelings were not Eliot's strong point. And yet—and yet—how worried he had been about disappointing his father! What a strange contradiction he was!

'I think we'll have to play it by ear when we arrive,' he said. 'Dad's memory isn't at all that good since he had his illness, so we should get away with it. Anyway, I'm sure he'll be charmed by you.'

He was looking at his watch as he threw in that last remark, so Fleur didn't think it needed acknowledgement.

'Now I'd better get the car out and get along to my office,' he said. 'I've several things to clear up there—

things I had to leave when I rushed away on Friday, with the optimistic idea that I was going to get married.' His lip twisted. Irony was beginning to replace any deeper show of emotion, and that was probably as good a defence as any, Fleur thought. For herself, she found that by now she could shrug off the memory of Roger without much difficulty.

Eliot stood up and surveyed her with a small frown. 'What will you do with yourself while I'm away? There are plenty of books and records——'

Fleur looked out of the window. 'I could go for a walk along the Embankment——' she began, but he interrupted her sharply.

'No, I'd rather you didn't go out.'

Her eyes widened with amazed disbelief. 'For heaven's sake! I've been in London on my own for three years. I'm perfectly capable of looking after myself.'

'Probably, but I would still prefer you to stay here.' His mouth had set stubbornly.

She was on the verge of arguing with him and then, suddenly, she understood. He couldn't face the possibility of being let down again, of coming back and finding she wasn't there.

'I shan't run away, you know,' she said quietly.

His mouth relaxed. 'Thank you,' he said, equally quietly, and she knew that the beginning of an understanding had taken root between them. It was a good feeling.

'I may be away some time,' Eliot said. 'I left a lot of stuff unfinished. At least there won't be anyone else there to interrupt me as it's Sunday morning, and I'll get back

as soon as I can. Then we'll pick up a late lunch somewhere and go on to Mandy's boutique afterwards, OK?'

Fleur smiled cheerfully. 'OK.'

He put a hand briefly on her shoulder. 'You're a grand
girl, Fleur,' he said, and then he was gone.

She stood quite still, looking at the door that had
closed behind him. Then she put up a hand and touched
her shoulder where his hand had rested. He liked her—
genuinely liked her, she didn't doubt it. He had said she
was a nice girl, a grand girl, that she was lovely, that his
father would be charmed by her.

What did all that add up to? Nothing, Fleur told
herself practically. Nothing at all. And she went across
to the hi-fi to select a record. Something as bracing and
unsentimental as she could find.

It was after two o'clock when Eliot returned. Fleur was
curled up on the sofa, re-reading *Paradise Postponed*,
and when the door opened she uncurled her legs and sat
up quickly, trying to ignore the way her pulses quickened
at the sight of the man, so crackling with vitality that
the whole room seemed to charge up like an electric
battery when he came in.

He walked across to her, his eyes very blue in the sunlight that poured in through the long windows. 'Sorry
I've been so long; have you been bored? And are you
starving with hunger?'

Fleur stood up. 'I couldn't be bored with all those
lovely records. I've played two of the Harrison
Birtwistles, Britten's *Ceremony of Carols*, and ended up
with *The Mikado*.'

'Hm—interesting mixture!' He looked upon her with approval. 'We must compare notes about music, I can see.'

'And as for the second question, yes, I'm definitely starving with hunger. I was tempted to raid the fridge, but that seemed rather pushy.'

'Pushy! My goodness, girl, you're the new mistress here, remember that. From now on you're Mrs Eliot Stevens. My cleaning lady, Mrs Frost, may be here in the morning before we leave for Heathrow. If so, you can practice on her.'

'Oh!' said Fleur rather blankly. It seemed that as soon as she managed to get more or less relaxed another challenge loomed up ahead.

'Don't worry, we'll cope,' Eliot said masterfully. 'We must remember to rumple up the bedclothes to make our wedding night look convincing.' Fleur felt the warmth creep into her cheeks, but he went on in the same practical voice, 'Oh, and by the way, while I was out I took the opportunity of contacting a good friend of mine who has an antique shop and getting him to take me along there. I managed to find these for you.' He felt in a pocket and drew out a small box. Inside was a narrow gold wedding-ring, chased in a lattice pattern, and worn almost paper-thin by the years. 'Georgian, I was told,' Eliot said. 'Try it on.' He picked up Fleur's left hand and slipped the ring on to her third finger. It fitted perfectly.

'And another.' He brought out a second box. 'Your engagement ring.'

An equally delicate ring of tiny diamonds and sapphires in a twisty filigree setting reposed on folds of black velvet inside. Eliot pushed it on to Fleur's finger beside the wedding-ring. 'There,' he said with satisfaction. 'That will help to remind you of your new status.'

She looked down at the two beautiful antique rings on her finger and had a disturbing feeling: what if it were real? If she were married to Eliot? She pushed the thought away. 'Thank you,' she said coolly. 'They're lovely, and they'll fill the bill for the time it takes to——' To what? She hadn't considered how long this pretence was to go on. 'We haven't set a time limit. How long are we to be married?'

Obviously Eliot hadn't thought about that either. He rubbed his cheek. 'We'll be in Italy a week; after that let's take it as it comes, shall we?' he said. Then he smiled, a warm, charming smile. 'You never know, little Fleur, we may like being married to each other so much that we decide to get married.'

The smile did terrible things to her composure, but she managed to sound unconcerned as she said, 'That's not very funny.' That, she thought, would make up for the snubs he had handed out to her!

Blue eyes glinted and she saw that the shot had gone home. But he chose to ignore it. 'Come on, let's go and eat,' he said, leading the way to the door.

They walked to a small Italian restaurant in the King's Road, where the proprietor, Mario, greeted Eliot like an old friend. Eliot spoke to him in fluent Italian, some of which Fleur could guess at. Mario's much more rapid replies were more difficult, but she gathered that the gist of it was: no, of course Il Signor Stevens was not too late for lunch. He was welcome at any time of the day or night. The day's speciality pasta was still 'on' and would be served *in fretta*.

Mario departed with a wide grin, the pasta arrived within five minutes and very good it was too. Fleur chased the final black olive round her plate, and refused a second glass of red wine. 'I need a clear head if I'm going to choose a trousseau; it'll be a new experience for me and I mean to make the most of it.'

'You didn't get as far as a trousseau with Roger, then?' Eliot asked idly, raising a finger to the waiter to order coffee.

Fleur thought quickly. She must make this sound convincing. 'Only as far as dreaming about it,' she told him with a deeply regretful sigh.

He was looking hard at her. 'I know the feeling. At least we can be completely honest with each other, and that's a good start.'

The waiter arrived with their coffee and Fleur welcomed the interruption. Eliot Stevens confused her and—she had to admit—disturbed her, but she mustn't let him know that, and she wasn't at all sure that she was going to be able to be completely honest with him in the days ahead.

The session at Mandy's boutique in Kensington was pure bliss. Never in her life had Fleur expected to have the money to buy an entire outfit of new clothes. And what clothes!

'Even in September it can still be very hot in Italy,' Mandy assured her. 'You have to be prepared for anything, Fleur.'

Mandy's liquid black eyes were shining as she produced her wares. Stretch tubes, she insisted, were the thing to wear at beach or pool. 'So much more elegant than the bikini—and so much more sexy,' Mandy murmured, producing a selection of gorgeously coloured bits of soft, stretchy nothing which, she assured Fleur, fitted just how and where you wanted them to fit, leaving bare as much as you chose. 'Topless beaches,' murmured Mandy, grinning. 'Navy and white stripes for driving around, or if the sun goes in and you need to cover up. *So* trendy and very elegant with your beautiful hair.' Mandy touched Fleur's shining tawny curls. 'Yes, it *must* be navy and white.'

So navy and white it was—striped jersey sweaters, tight cotton leggings, long, long white cardigans and even a striped hat with tip-tilted brim. Fun clothes, but Fleur wasn't sure that she would be feeling like having fun.

The large travelling-case that Eliot had brought with them in the car was rapidly and expertly being filled by Mandy. Two brief cotton sundresses followed the tubes and the stripes. A two-piece for travelling, in taupe jersey with a wide cummerbund that made Fleur's waist look even slimmer than it was. Two silky, uncrushable dresses in vivid prints that would fit any occasion.

'And for that special evening,' Mandy crooned finally, 'we can choose from many elegant dresses.'

Fleur's head was spinning as Mandy pulled out one seductive garment after another, hanging them along a high rail. Finally Fleur agreed to try on a floaty chiffon affair in misty silver-grey with a camisole top and shoulder straps studded with tiny seed pearls.

'With your lovely hair it is perfect,' Mandy exclaimed, clapping her hands. 'For when you both feel romantic.'

'But Mandy—it's not *supposed* to be romantic.' Fleur gave a helpless little laugh. 'It isn't a real honeymoon, Eliot explained that to you.'

Mandy looked mysterious. 'But who knows? When Eliot sees you in this—ahah——!'

Fleur glanced quickly over her shoulder as if Eliot might be standing at the door listening, but of course he wasn't—he and Toby had gone off together to look at some old building down near the docks, which they had their eyes on for buying to renovate.

'No.' She shook her head firmly. 'There's nothing between Eliot and me—nothing except a business arrangement. And anyway, Eliot's not my type—we'd clash horribly.'

Mandy lifted her eyes to heaven. 'But think how lovely the making up would be.'

Fleur didn't want to think about it. Just thinking about making up a quarrel with Eliot made her inside stir uncomfortably. But when she stood in front of the long mirror with the chiffon swirling round her slim legs and her arms and shoulders ivory-smooth against the ruched grey folds of the bodice she thought, at least he won't be able to look at me down his nose and see me as the little flower-girl.

Further than that she could not, and would not, allow her imagination to go.

Mandy was packing the grey chiffon dress in swathes of tissue when the two men returned, pleased with their inspection of the dockland property. They stood about in the small boutique looking large and rather out of place until Mandy produced two small gold chairs and insisted they they sat on them. 'I don't want my beautiful stock ruined by two bulls in a china shop,' she giggled.

Fleur was looking a little pink and dishevelled after so much trying on of garments. She ran a comb through her curls and said, 'Mandy's a wizard at selling clothes. I'm afraid we've run up an enormous bill.' She looked uncertainly towards Eliot. 'I feel you didn't expect to spend so much, Eliot. And I still have to find shoes and undies.'

Eliot waved a careless hand. 'All part of the package deal, and my way of saying thank you. We'll pick up the bits and pieces in the morning before we leave for Heathrow.'

Toby grinned. 'Eliot's in generous mood this afternoon—he's fallen in love with a broken-down old grain store.'

And indeed Eliot's blue eyes were shining with excitement. 'It's wonderful—pure Victorian Gothic with the most fascinating display of ornamental brickwork. They really let themselves go in those days. You must see it, Fleur, you'll love it.'

Fleur felt a warmth spreading through her as he smiled into her eyes, including her so naturally in his pleasure and enthusiasm. She held her breath, smiling back at him, and for a moment it seemed to her that they were alone in the small boutique.

Then Toby broke in with, 'If you two girls have finished your fashion parade, Eliot and I have a plan to go back into the West End and treat ourselves to a slap-up dinner; what do you say?'

Mandy threw her arms round his neck and kissed him. 'Lovely!' She closed the top of the travelling-case and handed it to Eliot. 'Here are all the goodies, I hope you approve. Fleur looks smashing in them, I promise you.'

'I'm sure she does.' Eliot linked a friendly arm with Fleur's as they left the shop. 'She always looks smashing.'

Smashing! Another adjective to add to her collection, Fleur thought wryly as they all piled into Eliot's car. She remembered how his face had changed when he had thought of Melissa standing on the cliff with the wind blowing through her hair, and wondered what word he would use to describe her. Certainly not 'smashing', she thought rather forlornly.

She could see the way he was beginning to pigeonhole her. Fleur the nice girl. Fleur the good sort, the reliable friend. She had a bleak feeling that it might not be enough for her.

'That was a very good dinner,' Eliot stated, opening the door of the house in Chelsea some hours later. 'Toby and Mandy certainly help to brighten the atmosphere. They're like a couple of kids when they get together.' As they climbed the stairs together he added, 'But Toby's a first-rate architect. By the way, we didn't mention it, but he's going to do the Porthgurran job for me, so you and your mother will be seeing quite a lot of him in the future.'

'Oh, yes? Good,' Fleur said rather vaguely. Dinner had been an easy, sociable meal, but now she was alone with Eliot again the churned-up feeling in her stomach was back in force. She had to face the fact that just being with him, hearing his voice, seeing the rare smile that touched his mouth, had a terrible effect on her composure—something she hadn't reckoned on when she'd agreed to his plan. It was only a physical reaction, of course, because he exuded that force that attracted the opposite sex like a magnet. Perhaps she would get used to it and be able to ignore it when they had been together a little longer. She hoped so.

He switched on lights inside the flat and went across to the drinks cupboard. 'Nightcap?' he enquired, holding up a bottle.

'No, thanks, I had quite enough wine at dinner,' Fleur said, staying near the door.

'I probably had too much—to drown my sorrows, of course. Isn't that what rejected lovers are supposed to do? Remember the old poem—"Oh, what can ail thee, Knight at arms, alone and palely loitering?"' He gave a hollow laugh. 'Which won't stop me from drowning them again.' He poured out a stiff whisky and flopped into a chair, long legs spread out in front of him. 'Come and sit down, Fleur, and don't hover like that.'

Fleur eyed him doubtfully. 'I'm rather tired; I think I'd like to turn in right away.'

'Would you now? You wouldn't be suspecting that I've had far too much to drink and might get—er—ideas that you wouldn't go along with?' His smile mocked her.

'No, I wouldn't,' Fleur said sturdily. 'You promised me when you first put your great plan to me that you weren't—in the mood for dalliance—I think was the way you put it, and I believed you. It may have been stupid of me to trust a complete stranger, but I did and I still do. I must, mustn't I?' she ended rather shakily. 'Otherwise the situation will be impossible.'

He had put down his glass and was regarding her with narrowed eyes, the mockery gone. Then he said slowly and ruefully, 'After that, all I can say is I'll try to deserve your good opinion of me, little Fleur. I only wish my opinion of myself were equally good.' He got to his feet. 'OK, if you feel like bed, so be it. We'll go and sort out some blankets and things.'

There was a commodious linen cupboard in the hall and Eliot fished out a couple of blankets and threw them on to the long sofa in the living-room. In the bedroom he took two pillows from the four on the double bed and a green towelling robe from the built-in closet. 'That's all I'll be needing for now,' he said. 'It's all yours.' He turned back the soft, fluffy quilt. 'Yes, Mrs Frost has provided whiter-than-white sheets for the bridal couple.' There was a little silence then he added bitterly, 'There's no end to rubbing salt into the wound, it would seem.'

Fleur glanced up at him. His face was stony; only the twisted mouth betrayed how much he was hurting inside. For the first time she saw that he had been putting on an act all day, and only now did she fully realise how mortally wounded he was by Melissa's rejection.

She touched his arm in a fleeting gesture. 'Goodnight, Eliot,' she whispered.

He nodded in silence and went out of the room.

It wasn't until their plane was airborne over the English Channel next day that Fleur began to find her tension easing away. There had been a subtle change in Eliot too, ever since they had stepped on to the plane at Heathrow. Some of the bitterness seemed to have gone

out of him. Perhaps he felt he was leaving a painful episode behind him for good as he left England. Whatever
the reason, Fleur welcomed the change. She lifted her
eyes from the stack of magazines he had bought for her
at the airport and glanced up at him, and he caught her
look and smiled.

'We're on our way now, Fleur,' he said softly. 'No
turning back.'

'Who said anything about turning back?' she retorted, straightening the skirt of her taupe jersey suit.
It was amazing how much confidence was built into new,
expensive clothes. She felt like a million dollars sitting
here in a luxurious first-class cabin with the best-looking
man on the plane beside her. 'What's our route when
we get to Nice?'

'We drive straight to our hotel in San Remo,' he told
her. 'I've been in the process of buying a new car and
I've arranged to have it delivered to me at the airport
when we arrive. We could go by the motorway, but I
think we'll take the Corniche instead—not so quick but
much more interesting.'

'A new car—what a thrill! What make?' Fleur enquired amiably. Not that she expected to be much wiser
if he told her. But he only grinned smugly and said, 'Wait
and see.'

When they emerged from the airport at Nice she saw
the reason for Eliot's smugness. The car waiting for him
was every man's dream car, a white Ferrari, glossily sleek
and utterly beautiful. The driver who delivered it, a
voluble Frenchman, was almost lyrical about the car as
he went through the paperwork with Eliot. Eliot's
expression was dead-pan until the driver had departed,

but, sitting behind the wheel of the exquisite machine as it purred effortlessly along the Middle Corniche, he allowed himself to gloat a little, manlike, over his new toy.

'I've been yearning for one of these for ages. Super, isn't she? What do you think?'

'Super,' agreed Fleur. She glanced up at the man beside her, his skin very bronzed, his black hair ruffled, his eyes blue as the sea far below, and glittering with enthusiasm. Her breath caught in her throat; he really was the most devastatingly attractive man! How could that girl Melissa ever walk out on him? She might have been sitting here now, in this fabulous car, married to this fabulous man, who adored her.

Ah, well, her loss is my gain, Fleur told herself, her lips quirking. *She* wasn't married to the man, and he certainly didn't adore *her*, but apart from those small details the days to come had the makings of a delightful holiday and she was determined to make the most of it.

A little smile played about her mouth as she laid her head back and relished the feel of the sun on her bare arms and the luxurious smell of new leather. The hood was down and the warm breeze whipped through her curls, and all around rose and fell the most wonderful scenic beauty she could ever imagine.

The colours were like no colours she had seen before and a succession of breathtaking views plunged down to the sea. Here a little village perched on a rocky spur that reached out into the deep blue water, there a curving harbour where sailing-boats rocked at anchor; and, looking upwards into the blue arc of the sky, the endless rising and dipping of the hills into the distance. Once, through a gap in the hills, she could even see far-off snow-capped peaks.

'What a glorious spot!' There was a lilt of pure pleasure in Fleur's voice. 'I think this is probably paradise—or one of its suburbs.'

Eliot took his eye off the busy road momentarily to glance down at the girl beside him, her tawny curls shining, her green eyes dancing with pleasure.

The straight line of his mouth softened. 'You've never been in these parts before?'

'Goodness, no. Much too exclusive for a poor student. I had a week in Paris with a party from the university in the Easter holidays and that's all I know of France, and I've never been to Italy at all. We had to visit Germany and Holland as part of the course, but it wasn't at all like this.'

'You're not sorry you came—now?' Eliot's voice was teasing. 'Not having regrets?'

'Regrets are a waste of time when you've made up your mind to do something, don't you think? No, I'm not having regrets, and so long as your plan works to give your father a little happiness, I'm going to enjoy every moment of my dream holiday before I go back home to the reality of hard work.'

'I think I shall enjoy it too,' Eliot said, and there was a hint of surprise in his voice. 'Yes, I'm sure I shall.'

Suddenly Fleur was engulfed in a cloud of confused and conflicting thoughts. What if this paradise worked its magic? What if they fell in love with each other?

Then she remembered Eliot's voice saying bitterly, 'I'll just have to be careful not to make the same mistake again.' Of course he wouldn't fall in love with her, and she mustn't allow this romantic Riviera background to fill her with foolish dreams. That way she would spoil what might be a wonderful holiday. She had to remember that everything Eliot had planned here was planned with the prospect of having Melissa beside him. Melissa, that exquisite girl with whose beauty she, Fleur, could never hope to compete.

She was reminded of this even more tellingly when they had gone through Passport Control and Customs and crossed the border into Italy, finally arriving at their journey's end, a dream of a hotel, cream-painted and red-roofed, set against a glorious backdrop of trees—olive and eucalyptus and cypress—above and beyond the harbour in San Remo. Flowers rioted in profusion around paved walks. Small tables were dotted about under the trees. Bougainvillaea hung in lush purplish-pink tresses from a pergola that led tantalisingly round a corner where the edge of a swimming pool could be glimpsed. Undoubtedly Eliot had chosen this place as the perfect setting for Melissa. It was so beautiful, just as she was, and it had about it an air of opulence that promised luxury and ease. Perfect for a honeymoon.

I won't think about Melissa, I won't, I *won't*, she told herself and as Eliot came round and opened the car door for her she laughed and said, 'Now I know I'm in paradise.'

'I don't know about paradise,' he told her, as a liveried servant came out to take their bags from the car, 'but I think we'll be comfortable here. You're a historian, you might be interested in the house's history. It was built by a Russian nobleman who was fleeing the Bolsheviks after World War I. It must have changed hands several times, but the present owners took it over about ten years ago and made it into a hotel. We used to come for a meal sometimes, when my parents first moved to these parts. I've always promised myself that one day I'd stay here, so it was the first hotel I thought of when I was planning the honeymoon.'

So casual! So matter-of-fact! She didn't know how he *could*. If it had been me that had been left standing at the altar, Fleur thought, I'd never want to refer to it, I'd want to shy away from any mention of it, anything that would remind me. He must be very, very confident to be able to bounce back as he seemed to be doing. Ah, well, she thought as they were greeted by a pretty, dark receptionist and borne upwards in the lift, it will make life much easier if I don't have to bother about sparing his feelings. And for some reason it was gratifying that he had chosen the hotel because he'd always intended to give it a try—not because of Melissa. Well, not exactly.

Their two bedrooms were on the first floor with wrought-iron balconies looking down across the tops of the trees, through which glimpses of the blue Mediterranean shone like jewels. 'Which room would you like?' Eliot said. 'Any preference?'

Fleur wandered from one room to the other. They were as she had imagined Italian rooms would be—cool and marble-floored, the furniture traditional—dark wood, lovingly polished and ornately carved, the rugs and curtains and bedspreads rich with subtle patterns. The huge bed in the larger of the two rooms had swathes of gold grapes modelled round its posts. The walls of both rooms were panelled, with flower murals painted in the recesses, delicate pink carnations in one room, sprays of yellow mimosa in the other.

'I think I'd better have the mimosa one,' she said lightly. 'It goes better with my hair.' She felt a little overcome with the size and faintly exotic atmosphere of the bedrooms, especially the king-size of the beds. She walked across to the gold-framed mirror on the dressing-table to push her curls into some kind of shape after their windswept journey.

But of course the rooms were no novelty to Eliot. When she turned, straightening up, he was standing close in front of her. 'You have very pretty hair, Mrs Stevens.' He took a shining russet strand between finger and thumb, and twisted it round. 'And when you smile you have a dimple in your right cheek.'

'Thank you,' she said coolly. He was too close for comfort, and when he had called her Mrs Stevens her heart had given a jolt and was thumping so hard that she felt sure he must hear it. 'Perhaps you'll give me a reference when this job's over?' she added, and then bit her lip because that had sounded stupidly flippant.

He said gravely, 'I should need more detailed knowledge of all the attractions that aren't immediately on view. And that I am not going to get, am I?'

'No way,' Fleur said. 'That was part of the original agreement. Now, will you bring my bag in here, please? It's degrees hotter than London, isn't it? And I really must discard some clothes.'

'I shan't have any grumbles if you discard them all,' Eliot said, dark blue eyes dancing wickedly.

She felt her cheeks go hot. 'Aren't you overdoing the loving husband role? There's nobody here to impress, you know.'

His grin widened. 'Just practising. It gets easier all the time to think of you as my wife. How is it with you? Can you see me as a loving husband yet?'

'I'm working on it,' she said coolly. 'Now may I pass, please?'

'Of course, *darling*.'

He leaned down and touched his mouth to the top of her shining head, and for a mad, shocked moment she wanted to reach up and draw his mouth down to hers. He moved away and she almost fell over, her knees sagging like stretched elastic. She grabbed the dressing-stool and sank on to it, turning to the mirror.

'My bag, please,' she mumbled, her back to him, and she knew by the way he moved away, slowly, reluctantly, that he too had been aware of the tension between them.

He brought her travelling-bag from the next room and dumped it beside the bed. Then he went across and opened a door on the far side of the room. 'Shower's in there. Come down when you're ready. We'll have a drink and then you'll have to excuse me for a while. I think it might make things easier if I go and visit my dad alone first and find out how he is, and how things are going with him.' He spoke easily, but she could sense the tension in him, the fear of what he might find when he saw his father again.

'Yes, of course,' she agreed immediately. 'Good idea.'

'And I can do a little tactful probing and find out exactly what I've already told him about my——' he hesitated '—my new wife. Then I can brief you so that everything should go smoothly and easily. Don't be too long, my sweet.' He leaned down and she felt the pressure of his lips warm on the back of her neck. 'Just practising again,' he murmured, and went quickly out of the room.

Fleur sat staring at herself in the mirror. Smoothly and easily? For him, perhaps. Already she could see the way things were going. He was going to rely on his power of attraction to get her into his bed. Very subtly, of course; he wouldn't rush her. But it wouldn't mean anything to him except a passing need, a passing pleasure, a way of restoring his male ego.

She hadn't thought of this—she hadn't worked things out far enough. She hadn't expected to respond to his sex appeal; she had vaguely imagined that she would go on thinking him arrogant and self-satisfied and chauvinistic and all the things she had thought him at first. She had taken it for granted that her first opinion of him would be enough to insulate her from his charms. Now she was facing the fact that it wouldn't. In fact, she was having to revise her first opinion of him altogether.

It was worrying. It made a tricky situation even more difficult. Because Fleur was firmly resolved not to let this mock honeymoon turn into what could only be a shallow, casual affair. Which, without love, it was bound to be.

Because Eliot was still in love with Melissa, and that wasn't going to change in a hurry.

CHAPTER SIX

BY THE time Eliot returned, the afternoon heat was going out of the sun. Fleur had unpacked and hung up all her lovely new clothes in the closet, explored the grounds of the hotel and finally settled in a lounger, alone on the terrace. A few guests were either lying round the swimming pool or lazily cutting their way through the green water. The hotel was small and some of them would probably be friendly, but just now Fleur didn't feel like meeting new people.

She saw Eliot coming towards her and felt her stomach squeeze up at the sudden sight of him, big and bronzed and handsome in white trousers and a dark blue shirt, open at the neck.

'You look comfy—recovered from the travelling?'

He leaned down and kissed her lightly, and she wondered if he really needed to rehearse his role quite so often. She was finding that his touch increased her heartbeat in a most disturbing manner.

'How did you find your father?' she asked, drawing away quickly in case he thought it necessary to get too enthusiastic.

'I was relieved. I thought he seemed to have a little more vitality than when I last saw him. Luisa—that's the housekeeper, who looks after him—says he's been eating better these last few days. Apparently he's talked about nothing but our visit.'

112

He dropped into the lounger beside her, reaching out to cover her hand with his. 'My dear, I can't tell you how grateful I am to you. It would have been the most difficult thing in my life to confess to him what actually happened.' His voice was deep with sincerity; he wasn't role-playing any longer.

'I'm glad,' she said slowly. 'And I'll do my best—when am I to see him?'

'At the first possible moment. He says he's always wanted a daughter, and he can't wait to see you. I'm to take you back with me straight away and Luisa is going to fix a meal for us.'

Fleur got to her feet. 'Will I do like this, or should I change into something more formal?' She was wearing a sleeveless sundress in a pretty Laura Ashley print.

Eliot stood up and his blue eyes gleamed with approval as he looked her up and down. 'You look delicious.' He ran his hand up her bare arm and she flinched away at his touch.

'Don't,' she gasped.

His dark brows went up. 'Fleur—what *is* this? You're not going to let me down, are you? I have to touch you now and then, you know, or we're not going to convince anyone.'

Fleur's confusion was real enough, but she couldn't confess to him that the feel of his fingers on her arm had started a fire smouldering deep inside her. 'I'm—I'm sorry,' she stammered. 'You took me by surprise.'

He was looking oddly at her, frowning slightly. 'What is it with you, girl? Do you dislike being touched?'

'N-no,' she mumbled. 'It isn't that. It was—it was—oh, I don't know,' she finished irritably. 'Don't let's go on about it.'

He shrugged, but he still looked faintly worried. 'Dad will expect us to be love-birds.'

She turned towards the door into the lounge. 'I've said I'll do my best,' she said shortly. 'I'll go up and get my bag and a wrap.'

He was beside her as she reached the bottom of the stairs, and walked up behind her. When she went into her room he followed her and shut the door.

'Look,' he said heavily, 'we must work this out before we go any further. Tell me truly, do you really object to my touching you—kissing you? Is it because I'm not Roger, or because I'm me? I must know, because if I really turn you off we'd better cancel the whole thing here and now. I'd rather go and confess to my father and hope he'd understand than have him wondering if I've made a mistake. He hasn't had much joy from his own marriage to my stepmother, and he's hoped for something better for me—I know that. If we can't convince him that we're in love, then the whole thing falls flat.'

She looked at him, leaning his back against the door, blue eyes regarding her uncertainly under long, dark lashes, and thought—he expects the truth and this is where I start to lie. If I told him the truth, if I said, just looking at you turns my bones to water, I wonder what he'd say. He would certainly think she wanted some deeper involvement, possibly even suspect that she was trying to pull that old trick—to catch him on the rebound. If she confessed that she was in danger of falling in love with him, he'd be horrified. She bit her lip. Why was life so complicated for women—why couldn't they just take lovemaking as a pleasant interlude, as men did? Perhaps some women could—she certainly couldn't.

She turned away and walked to the window, looking down over the tops of the trees to the glimpses of sea far below. She said in a muffled voice, 'I've been silly and it's just because I feel so—so strange in this situation. And no—I don't object to your touching me.' She could have added, and heaven only knows, you certainly don't turn me off—quite the reverse. Only of course she didn't.

'Well, I must say that's a relief.' He didn't move from where he was standing with his back to the door. 'Fleur.'

'Yes?' She still looked out of the window.

'Come over here.'

Something in his voice sent little thrills shooting through her. She turned and walked slowly towards him, putting a composed, enquiring little smile on her lips.

He still didn't move. 'Closer,' he said softly.

Their bodies were almost touching as she stood before him. 'Now prove it,' he said. 'Put your arms round me and kiss me.'

Suddenly she was trembling, the heat inside her beginning to smoulder like a furnace fanned into life. Of their own volition her hands went up round his neck and drew his head down. She put her mouth against his and let it rest there passively for a moment. Then the feel of him against her, the moulded softness of her against his hard, taut body was too much for her. Her lips parted and she let out a little gasp of excitement.

He covered her mouth with his, his tongue caressing her lips. One hand slipped the strap of her sundress down over her arm and his fingers closed over the tender swell of her breast, squeezing gently until she almost screamed with mounting desire as he moved rhythmically against her. No man had ever had this devastating effect on her before. She wanted him, she wanted the ecstasy that she guessed he could give her. Her body arched itself against him.

His mouth left hers. Very gently he put her away from him and pulled up the shoulder-strap of her dress.

'That,' he said huskily, 'was a very convincing demonstration. Now, let's go, shall we, before we both get carried away? Playing with fire's a dangerous game. We'll have to handle it carefully.'

Indeed we will, Fleur thought, following him out to the car. She'd been almost lost then, willing him to do as he liked with her. And it wasn't her style. Sex without love was something that went against her deepest convictions. He didn't love her and wasn't likely to. And she didn't love him, did she? The danger was there, she knew that only too well, but knowing the danger was half-way to overcoming it. She just had to be very, very careful.

In the car he said, 'I think we're home and dry about the information I gave in my letters to my father. I did a bit of probing, and it seems that all he knows about the girl I was going to marry was that she was living in Cornwall and that I'd met her in the course of business. I'm pretty sure I told him more, but if I did he couldn't have taken it in. It all happened so quickly, and I'm not much of a letter writer.'

'So——' Fleur said thoughtfully, 'I can tell him about my own background truthfully, if he asks me. That's a relief.' She had noted that this time he said 'the girl I was going to marry' and not 'Melissa'. For some obscure reason that pleased her.

In the car he said, 'I did tell Dad a little about you—and your mother, and the flower shop—but I don't think he took very much of it in.' In the fading light she saw his mouth twitch as he steered his way carefully along the harbour road among the press of cars, all of which seemed to her to be driving far too fast and sounding their horns in a wild frenzy. 'That, at any rate, tallied with what I must have told him before—that we'd met in the course of business.'

'Yes, we did, didn't we?' Fleur said smoothly. 'And you were beastly to me. We certainly didn't fall in love at first sight.'

He grimaced. 'I'm sorry about that. I had a lot on my mind just then, and you looked such a kid in your jeans and that skimpy green top.'

So he'd remembered what she was wearing! Fleur felt a rush of pure pleasure.

'I admit I got quite a shock when I heard you tell Mrs Templeton that you were twenty-two. I was impressed by the way you stood up to that woman—and when we encountered each other again I was even more impressed. Everything about you suggested that you had guts, my child, and that's what gave me the nerve, finally, to put my outrageous suggestion to you.'

The car turned off the main coast road and climbed up a twisting road into the hills, passed through a small village and soon turned in between wrought-iron gates and slid to a halt. 'Talking of nerves,' Fleur said in a shaky voice, '*my* nerves are dancing a rumba at the moment. I haven't felt like this since my final exams.'

Eliot switched off the engine and squeezed her hand hard. 'And I'm willing to bet you'll pass this exam, too. With honours,' he added. 'If you get stuck or feel at sea about anything, just look at me and I'll improvise.' He got out and opened the car door for her with a flourish.

Fleur was in no state to take in details, but in the evening light she saw that the villa was the colour of yellow ochre and half smothered in climbing plants. The garden that sloped down from the front drive was rocky and that, too, was lush and overgrown. As she followed Eliot to the front door the scent of damp plants and the constant chirp of cicadas filled the cool air.

Inside, Fleur was conscious immediately of the quietness. Crossing the marble-tiled hall she put a hand, almost instinctively, into the crook of Eliot's arm. He looked down at her and gave her hand an encouraging squeeze. Then he threw open a door on the left of the hall and cried, 'Here we are, Dad,' and she was being led across a large, square room, to a chair in the window where Eliot's father was sitting.

Geoffrey Stevens got slowly to his feet and stood waiting for them. He was very tall, very thin, and pitifully frail, but as soon as he smiled Fleur's fears were forgotten. His eyes were as blue as his son's eyes. Time and illness had faded them, but when he smiled they lit up and little crinkles fanned out at the corners.

He didn't wait for Eliot to present her. He held out his arms and said, 'My dear girl—this is a great day for me.'

She went into his arms and he kissed her on both cheeks and held her away, gazing at her with obvious delight.

'For me, too,' she said, and, oddly enough, knew it to be true. She had believed that it was only for the sake of saving her mother's flower shop that she had agreed to Eliot's plan, but now she knew that the warm pleasure she was feeling was an important bonus.

'Sit down, sit down, and let me look at you.' Mr Stevens settled himself in his big chair again. It looked well worn and comfortable, but Fleur guessed that he spent most of his day in it—which was a pity, she thought. She wondered if she could lure him out of it while she was here.

Eliot drew up a small sofa and pulled Fleur down on to it with him, very close. Keeping an arm round her, he grinned and tipped her face up to his. 'What do you think, Dad?' he grinned. 'Isn't she gorgeous? Isn't she just as lovely as I told you?'

'Lovelier,' his father said with his slow, crinkly smile.

'There, what did I tell you, sweetheart?' Eliot planted a kiss on Fleur's lips before he released her chin. And to his father, 'Do you know, Dad, the girl's been jittery about meeting you. So anxious to make a good impression! The vanity of these women!' He raised his eyes to heaven.

'Don't believe a word of it, Mr Stevens,' Fleur put in indignantly, and he smiled and said,

'Oh, I don't, my dear. But please don't call me Mr Stevens. How does Dad sound? Or Geoffrey? Or Daddy? Or is that too deb-like?'

'I think Dad sounds super.' She glanced towards Eliot, wondering what he had told his father about her parents.

'Fleur's father died when she was a baby, I don't know if I told you, Dad,' Eliot said, and she put in,

'So now I'll have a father, after all these years.'

'And I'll have a daughter, which is something every man hopes for. You've arranged it very neatly, Eliot, my boy.' He turned to Fleur. 'But there's just one thing I don't quite understand. I thought your name was Melissa, my dear.'

Fleur went cold. This was something that neither of them had thought of. She lifted her eyes to Eliot's. Let him get her out of this one.

He didn't hesitate for a moment. 'That's easily explained, Dad. Her mother has an abiding passion for flowers—hence the nickname.'

She slid him a look which only the two of them would be able to interpret. Mr Cleverboots, the look said quite plainly.

But she entered into the spirit of the thing. 'I've always been Fleur for as long as I can remember,' she said truthfully. 'I think my darling mother imagined I'd grow up into a beautiful English rose. What a disappointment!' She shook her tawny curls, laughing.

'There are other beautiful flowers,' Eliot put in, running a finger down her cheek. 'Tiger lilies, for instance.'

'Fierce, am I?' She pretended to growl horribly, and snapped at his finger, biting it quite hard between white, even teeth. It was a pleasurable experience, she wasn't quite sure why. She didn't really want to hurt him, although she had a feeling that she needed to keep up her own end—not to let him take her too much for granted. But the taste of his skin against her lips sent a tingle down her spine and she released his finger quickly.

'That was most uncalled-for,' he said sternly, his eyes dancing with amusement. 'But I have a very good method of taming the wild beast.' He leaned over and kissed her full on the mouth.

His father chuckled. 'Well done, son. I can see you two are going to have a highly enjoyable honeymoon.' The faded eyes rested almost sadly on Fleur's flushed cheeks. Was he remembering, perhaps, his own honeymoon—had things started to go wrong as early as that? She felt a squeeze of compassion.

The door opened then and a small, dark woman in a black dress and a voluminous white overall, her hair scraped into a bun on top of her head, came in and stood just inside it. 'Dinner is served, Mr Stevens,' she announced, and her black eyes went to Fleur with undisguised interest.

'Luisa—come and meet my new daughter,' Geoffrey Stevens invited and the housekeeper padded across the room, smiling widely.

'*Buona sera, signora*. It is so fortunate to meet you.'

Fleur stood up, holding out her hand. 'Lovely to meet you, Luisa. You speak very good English.'

Luisa's smile widened into a beam, white teeth gleaming. 'Ah, the Signor Stevens, he teach me. He tell me I good—good——?' She waved her hands in the air as if she could catch the word.

'Pupil?' Fleur tried.

'*Si, si*—pupil. Now, come and eat dinner, I make a splendid pasta and afterwards a roast and I buy *panforte sapori* for after dinner with coffee. I remember you like *panforte*, Signor Eliot.'

'Luisa, you're a genius.' Eliot stood up and held out a hand to his father. 'Come along, Dad, let's do justice to this wonderful celebration meal.'

He helped his father to his feet and Fleur noticed how shaky the older man was. But he passed it off with a grunt and a quip about old bones.

'Old!' Eliot scoffed. 'You—you're a mere lad of fifty-eight.' He took his father's arm affectionately.

'Certainly you are—Dad,' Fleur said stoutly, taking his other arm. And as the three of them walked across the room, laughing together, she felt that she had made a good beginning in her role as Eliot's new wife. His father had accepted her gladly and she need have no further fear on that count.

The fear that she was going to have to deal with, the fear that was growing more insistent every time her eyes met the vital blue gaze of her mock 'husband', was quite a different matter.

There was plenty to talk about as they ate Luisa's excellent dinner. Eliot had been sent to choose a bottle of wine and returned with a wide smile. 'I see you've stocked in with Barolo, Dad. My favourite.'

His father looked pleased. 'I thought you would have drunk enough champagne at your wedding and would welcome a change.'

'Good thinking.' Eliot was plying a corkscrew and didn't look up from the task.

'Now, you must tell me all about the wedding. I sat here all alone on Saturday imagining just what was happening and longing to be there with you. Cornwall's a place I always meant to visit and never got around to. I'm sure it's a very beautiful spot.'

Fleur glanced at Eliot, and when he didn't seem to be going to say anything she jumped into the breach herself. 'Oh, indeed it is. My mother is Cornish and I love the place. I suppose the coast is a tiny bit like your coastline here—lots of bays and harbours and rocky inlets. And it's so warm that palm trees actually grow there in places. And flowers, too.' She chattered on nervously, glancing again at Eliot. How much had he told his father about Melissa's parents? Or had he substituted information about her own? It was all so confusing. But he didn't help her, so she ventured on, 'My mother keeps a florist's shop on the quayside in Porthgurran—that's a small fishing town on the south coast. Did Eliot tell you?' Now he would *have* to come into the conversation.

The cork came out of the wine bottle with a plop. 'I think I did mention it in one of my letters, Dad,' Eliot said smoothly. 'That's how Fleur and I met—the company has bought an old quayside building that houses the shop, and we're planning to incorporate a bigger and better shop for my new mother-in-law when the alterations are done.'

His father was listening intently, nodding now and then. 'A flower shop—now that sounds fascinating. You must tell me all about it, my dear.'

Fleur felt a wave of relief. It was a signal to her that she could talk truthfully and naturally about herself. She didn't have to pretend to be Melissa, with rich parents and a luxurious home on a cliff-top. While they ate Luisa's excellent dinner the talk centred round flowers, which was a safe subject as well as a delightful one. Eliot didn't join in the conversation very much—he was watching Fleur and his father quite intently, and she wondered just what he was thinking. She hoped she was making a good impression on the older man and she believed she was, but no doubt she would be told later. Certainly, he wasn't giving her much help.

'San Remo has its own flower market—possibly the most famous in Italy. You must get Eliot to take you there in the early morning—the scent of the flowers is quite overwhelming.' Geoffrey Stevens's cheeks had a little colour in them now, and his eyes were brighter. He looked a different man from the one who had got up stiffly out of his chair when Fleur and Eliot came in. She hoped he wasn't getting too excited and that he wouldn't suffer for it later.

'And then, of course, there's the famous Hanbury Gardens at La Mortola—that's one thing you must see while you're here. You've been there, haven't you, Eliot?'

Eliot nodded. 'We'll add it to our honeymoon itinerary,' he said, smiling across the table at Fleur. 'We have yet to plan it in detail, haven't we, sweetheart?' he added, and he managed to infuse such warmth into his voice that she could feel herself responding. It was getting dangerously easy to believe, at times, that all this was real and not play-acting.

Geoffrey was describing the gardens to Fleur and how Sir Thomas Hanbury had bought the grounds with its old castle in the nineteenth century and created a fabulous garden with literally thousands of plants and trees from all over the world.

'I used to wander there for hours when we first came down here to live,' he went on, 'but now——' he

shrugged wryly '—I'm afraid it's out of bounds for me.
I couldn't manage the walking.' Suddenly he looked sad.
'I miss it very much.'

'Perhaps—when you are feeling better——?' Fleur
ventured, but the elderly man shook his head.

'I have to be content with my own garden here. But
even that is sadly neglected—labour isn't too easy to
come by.'

'We'll put it to rights for you while we're in these
parts,' Eliot offered. 'Won't we, darling?'

His father demurred, 'Oh, you won't want to spend
your honeymoon weeding an overgrown garden, son.'

Fleur jumped in immediately. 'We'd love to, Dad,' she
said. 'I'm an absolute wizard with weeds, and I've been
starved of gardens while I've been studying in London.'

The talk turned to her years at university and her
chosen subject of art history. 'You've come to the right
spot,' Geoffrey told her enthusiastically. 'Liguria has attracted many famous artists. I've got lots of books you
could read——'

Eliot was grinning wickedly. 'I'm afraid, Dad, I'm not
going to give Fleur much time for reading.'

His father chuckled understandingly and Fleur
blushed, and thought how ridiculous it was that she
should do so, but she couldn't help it. This whole situation was turning into something of a farce, but at least
Eliot's father was quite patently enjoying himself, and
that, she told herself, was what it was all about.

They drank their coffee on the terrace and ate slices
of *panforte sapori*—a delicious, chewy, flat cake made
of nuts and fruits and spices. Moths flew round and in-
sects chirruped and damp evening scents came up to them

from the rocky garden that clung to the hillside below the house. They didn't talk much now and Fleur had a feeling of being at ease, as if she were sitting here with a familiar and well-loved family, and not two strangers. It was very odd, but very pleasant. Soon, however, the evening grew too cool to sit outside and Geoffrey admitted being a little tired.

'I think I should perhaps seek my bed,' he confessed. 'I retire early these days. You two have been very sweet and unselfish to share your first evening here with an ailing old man, who has enjoyed it more than he can say. You'll come up with me, son? Goodnight, my dear new daughter, and come again soon.' He kissed Fleur affectionately.

'We certainly will,' Fleur promised. 'I'm looking forward to that weeding.' She saw Eliot nod and felt a tingle of pleasure. The meeting had gone off well, better than she could have imagined.

Eliot didn't say much on the drive back to the hotel. He slipped a cassette into the stereo and kept his eyes on the road ahead. Fleur didn't want to talk. She laid her head back against the soft leather of the seat and enjoyed the Mozart piano music and dreamily watched the trees above as the lights from passing cars lit rustling leaves with a ghostly whiteness. She was enjoying herself. She had had a good dinner, perhaps a little too much of the red wine called Barolo, and she reckoned she had come through the meeting with Eliot's father without a stumble. In short, she was feeling more than a little pleased with herself.

The hotel lounge was empty except for two elderly ladies who were sitting in front of a large TV screen.

One of them was busily knitting an anonymous strip of bright pink. 'Doesn't she look like Miss Marple?' Fleur whispered to Eliot, with a suppressed giggle.

'Hm?' He looked down at her absently.

'You know—Agatha Christie's detective.'

'Oh!' He glanced without interest at the couple, and went on walking towards the lift.

Fleur followed, conscious of a vague disappointment. She had thought that perhaps they might linger for a while to talk over a last drink. She had been expecting—looking forward to—Eliot's pleased reaction to the evening visit. Surely she deserved a word of approval for having got through it without any blunders? And his father had liked her—she was sure of it. That must please him, mustn't it?

If it did, he evidently wasn't going to tell her so. At the door of her room he stopped and unlocked it for her, handing her the key. 'You're ready to turn in?' he enquired politely, but didn't wait for her reply. 'We'll meet for breakfast at about half-past eight, or is that too early for you?'

She glanced up at his face, but it told her nothing of what he was thinking or feeling. 'No, of course half-past eight isn't too early.'

He nodded. 'Good, I'll see you then and we can arrange how we're going to pass the day.'

Pass the day? The way he said it he might have said, how we're going to *get through* the day. What was wrong? Fleur wondered, and then she knew, and she had to stifle a gasp because the knowledge was a sudden, sharp pain. Of course! Eliot had praised her, jollied her along, until the meeting with his father. He had produced his promised bride to his father and she had been accepted. In effect, her part in this charade was really over. He would have to pass a few days in her company, however much it bored him, however much he was longing for Melissa and remembering how it might have been. That was it, it must be. Nothing else could account for his sudden change of mood. She was surprised how much the knowledge hurt.

'Yes,' she said. Her face felt stiff with the effort of smiling. 'Goodnight, then, Eliot.'

'Goodnight, Fleur,' he said, and walked quickly back along the corridor, not stopping at the door of his own room. Evidently he was going down to the bar, but he had made it plain he didn't want her company.

Fleur went into her bedroom and closed the door with a sharp bang. If that was the way he wanted it, it was all right with her. She'd been idiotic to put a personal interpretation on the way he'd behaved; even more idiotic to let her feelings become involved in his family situation. He and his father were complete strangers and had no part in her life. His attitude towards her had been calculated from the very first moment he'd implored her help. She'd been stupid enough to let herself read all sorts of messages that hadn't been there. She'd even fallen into the trap of allowing herself to fancy him, because—she had to admit it—he was an extremely sexy man. How utterly, *utterly* pathetic!

She was shaking inside with hot anger—with herself, with him, with the whole ridiculous situation—as she pulled off her clothes and got into a flimsy wrap that was part of her 'trousseau', that Eliot had insisted on her buying in London before they left. 'Just so that you will feel like a bride,' he had persuaded her. 'You need to dress the part.'

To impress—who? The sales girl at Harrods? A hotel chambermaid? *Herself?* she fumed inwardly. Well, she certainly didn't feel like a bride, and she might as well have bought a sensible cotton and polyester dressing-gown at Marks and Sparks. That at least would fit in with her life-style when this stupid farce of a honeymoon was over.

She caught sight of her reflection in a long looking-glass on the wall, her cheeks flushed, her green eyes brilliant with indignation. No hope of going to sleep yet. But neither was she going to lie awake and think about Eliot Stevens. Certainly *not*, she told herself, rummaging in her bag for the magazines he had bought her at Heathrow.

The bed was large and blissfully comfortable. Fleur turned over the pages of the magazine slowly, one by one, reading everything including the advertisements. She read articles about fashion, beauty, health, travel, gardening. An hour later she wasn't aware of a single detail from any of them. She *was* aware, however, that there had been no sound from the room next door, of Eliot coming up to bed. So subconsciously she must have been listening for him. Damn the man, she thought, throwing the magazine on the floor in disgust.

As though it were an answer to her angry gesture, she heard a step on the marble floor of the corridor. There was a tap on the door and Eliot's voice said, 'Fleur—are you awake?'

She lay transfixed for a moment, deciding whether to admit it or to feign sleep and let him go away. It wasn't

a difficult decision. She leapt out of bed, padded to the
door, and opened it a crack. If he'd been drinking
downstairs for over an hour she might be unwise to open
it any further. But although he looked heavy-eyed and
pale beneath his tan, he certainly wasn't drunk.

'May I come in?' he said, his eyes travelling over her,
in her revealing pink wrap.

'I was in bed,' she said coldly. 'What do you want?'

He smiled faintly. 'Only to talk.'

'All right, then, I suppose you can.' She had to pretend
reluctance although she recognised, with alarm, that reluctance was the very last thing she was actually feeling.
Instead she felt suddenly alive and vibrant and ridicu-
lously happy. She'd been wrong about his not wanting
her company; he was here, asking to talk to her. It didn't
matter yet what he wanted to talk about, it was enough
that he was here, sitting back in an armchair, deep blue
eyes gleaming in the light from the bedside-lamp, wide
brow creased under rumpled black hair.

Fleur sat on the bed, arranging the wrap to cover her
feet, hugging her knees. 'Well?' she said brightly.

The silence that followed went on and on until she
could have screamed. His eyes were fixed on her face,
but she wondered if he were really seeing her—almost
he seemed to be looking straight through her and seeing
something else. Some*one* else? Melissa?

'Well?' she said again rather tartly when she couldn't
bear it any longer. 'Is there something special you wanted
to say to me, or is this merely a social call?'

'There is something rather special, as you put it. I've
been out in the garden, walking about, risking the
midges. And I've been thinking, Fleur. Thinking hard.'

Another pause. 'Yes?' she prompted.

'The first thing is to thank you for making the meeting with Dad a resounding success.' He smiled again, that faint, twisty smile. 'You've made a hit with him, that's for sure.'

'He made a hit with me,' Fleur said. 'He's a darling.'

He nodded slowly. 'Yes. It was an enjoyable occasion, a happy, family occasion.' He stopped and then added very wryly, 'Something quite new in my experience. As I've told you, Dad and I have always been close, but my family has been a threesome, and whenever I've been at home it's been——' he shrugged '——continual sniping, if not outright quarrelling. That's all I remember of family life, but this evening I saw what it might be. People liking each other, talking easily, sharing interests.'

'I enjoyed it too,' Fleur said. 'You don't have to thank me. I didn't do anything special.'

'That's what I want to say. You didn't have to do anything special. It was enough merely to be yourself, Fleur. And while I've been walking in the garden, the thought came to me that I'd be a prize idiot to lose a girl like you, a warm, kind girl. A girl who could make a happy home.'

Fleur's mind was spinning crazily. What was he saying? There seemed only one way to take it, but that was ridiculous, impossible. 'You seem to be taking an awful lot about me for granted,' she murmured. 'I might be putting on a great big act; I might be an absolute bitch.'

He got out of his chair and came and sat on the bed, near her—much too near. Her inside flipped as he smiled into her eyes. 'I know a bitch when I meet one. And I've learnt a lot about you in a short time. It's been a pretty fraught time. Don't the psychologists say one's perceptions are heightened at moments of crisis?'

'Do they? I'm not very well up in psychology,' Fleur said stiffly.

He smiled, as if that didn't surprise him. 'I expect you're wondering what all this is leading up to? I didn't want to spring it on you suddenly, but I can't see any other way. What I'm getting at, Fleur, is that I'd like to make our pretend marriage into a real one.'

She stared at him blankly. So it hadn't been ridiculous and impossible, it had been true. He was actually asking her to marry him. At least, she thought he was.

'This is a proposal? You're asking me to *marry* you?'

'Yes,' he said. 'Or if that's too startling all at once, I'm asking you to consider the idea.'

Fleur was suddenly more angry than she had ever been in her life. 'I never heard of anything so—so—why, it's insulting.' Her voice rose to a squeak. 'It's positively indecent, asking a girl to marry you when you're crazily in love with another girl. That's how you put it, wasn't it? Crazily in love. That's what you said to me in the cottage.'

'That's in the past,' he said calmly. 'I told you. I'm not crazy any more. I'm being more sensible than I've been for a long time.'

She shook her head. The man was incredible. 'Three days! Hardly long enough to transfer your—er—affections. Even on the rebound, as it's called.' Her lip curled in disdain.

'My dear girl,' he said patiently. 'I'm not talking about transferring my affections, as you call it. I'm not offering you undying love; I've seen where that kind of romantic nonsense leads to. It's been a short, sharp lesson but I've learned it thoroughly, I hope. You don't walk into the same trap twice, not if you're half-way sane, you don't. I won't pretend that it doesn't hurt still, but I'll get over it. In a week or two I'll have forgotten it ever happened.' He paused, frowning a little, then went on, 'I realise that I should have waited until that happened before asking you, but—as I explained—I didn't want to take the risk of you being snapped up by another man. You're a very attractive girl, Fleur.'

'You make me sound like something from a bargain basement,' she said bitingly. 'Buy early and avoid the rush!'

'I'm sorry,' he said. 'I didn't mean it like that. I'm just trying to be honest. You told me about Roger and how you were let down. I was—well, you know all about that. It seemed to me that we should be able to build one good thing out of two bad things.'

'Without the danger of any romantic nonsense?'

He looked sharply at her. 'Precisely.'

Fleur met his gaze squarely. He was sitting on the side of the bed, about level with her hunched knees, and she drew them up a little nearer to her body. 'I suppose I must thank you for your proposal, but I'm afraid I'm not accepting it. I happen to believe that marriage without the "romantic nonsense" would be a very cold and unsatisfactory affair.'

She saw him recoil. 'Cold?' In the shaded light his eyes glittered, narrowed. '*Cold?* Oh, no, not on your life.' He leaned towards her and grasped the hands that were hugging her knees, pulling them away until her legs straightened and she was lying flat on her back, staring up at him with wide eyes as he loomed over her.

He was going to kiss her and she wanted him to—oh, yes, she wanted it. But she couldn't risk it. She twisted round and pulled herself up straight against the back of the bed, as far away from him as she could get.

'You needn't bother to demonstrate,' she said coolly. 'You gave a very adequate demonstration before we left this evening. There's only one reason for marrying, I believe, and that's if two people are in love. As you and I certainly aren't in love, it would be simply for—for your convenience. And sex,' she added, and to her intense annoyance she heard her voice tremble. Damn it, she'd been congratulating herself on handling this situation with poise. Now she'd spoilt it. But perhaps he hadn't noticed.

Vain hope! The blue eyes were full of mockery and—something else that she couldn't put a name to. 'Dear little Fleur,' he said. He stood up and moved towards the door. 'I won't try to win you round to my way of thinking tonight, but I warn you, I'm not going to give up the idea. Goodnight, Fleur. We'll discuss it another time.'

CHAPTER SEVEN

'THANK goodness!' Janet's worried voice came loud and strong over the phone from Miami on Tuesday night. 'My darling child, what *have* you been getting yourself into? Your letter came this morning, and Brenda and I have been biting our nails with sheer nerves all day. Fleur, pet, what is it all about and are you all right and where are you?' The words tripped over themselves with an energy that Janet hadn't shown for a long time. When she had left England she'd been very quiet and subdued. The life-style of Aunt Brenda in the US had certainly been doing wonders for her.

'I'm fine, Mum. I'm having a super holiday on the Italian Riviera and everything is going along splendidly, according to the plan I wrote you about.' She glanced over her shoulder, but Eliot, who had instigated the call to Miami, had tactfully retired from her room when it came through.

'But, my dearest girl, you shouldn't have taken a risk like that for my sake—no flower shop in the world is worth it,' Janet wailed. 'Why, you hardly knew the man. He might have been—have been——' Words failed her.

Fleur laughed. 'Well, he wasn't, and he isn't, so set your doubts aside. He's the most delightful person, and his father—for whose sake this whole plan was invented—is a pet. We've spent the whole day today with him, helping to set his garden to rights. He has a won-

derful garden, Mum, you'd love it. Steep and rocky—
there aren't any lawns in these parts—and full of unusual flowers. We've just got back to our hotel in San
Remo in time for dinner.'

There was a short silence at the other end of the line.

'Yes, Mum, I know what you're thinking, and we *do*
have separate rooms.' Before Janet had time to ask any
questions she hurried on, 'I can't explain any more now,
Mum. I suppose it seems crazy to you, but I had to use
my judgement about the whole thing, and I decided to
go through with it. And that's all I can tell you. So you
mustn't worry any more about me, and very soon we'll
be together again at home, planning your super new
shop.'

Janet said more slowly, 'I must admit it sounds exciting, and I'm intrigued. Have you checked on what's
happening at the shop while you're away? This secretary
person—is she coping?'

'I'm sure she is, Mum. Eliot rang her this morning
and she seems to have everything running smoothly. She's
terrifyingly efficient. You'll probably find your
bookwork in apple-pie order when you get back.'

'That'll be a nice change.' Her mother's warm chuckle
came over the line, and it was good to hear it. Janet
hadn't laughed for quite a long time.

'Have you decided yet when you'll come back?' Fleur
asked.

There was a pause, then Aunt Brenda's voice came.
'Fleur, you bad child! You've always been too impulsive
for your own good!' But Fleur could imagine the smile
on her aunt's round, good-natured face. 'Your mother's
getting better by the hour, and I'm insisting she stays on

here for a few more days. Her shop seems to be in good hands from what you say—and if there are going to be changes and re-building there's no earthly reason for her to rush back.'

The call continued for a few more minutes. Phone numbers of the hotel in San Remo and Geoffrey's villa were supplied, together with more reassurance and loving messages.

'Goodbye for now, Mum. Look after yourself.' Fleur was smiling as she replaced the receiver and went to find Eliot in his room next door. As she came in, he got up from one of the two comfortable chairs. Dark eyebrows raised, he enquired, 'Well, how did it go?'

'I think I managed to satisfy her that I hadn't gone bonkers,' Fleur told him, sinking into the second chair, still smiling. 'And that you were honourable and trustworthy—a pillar of society, in fact.'

'Oh, dear!' Eliot grimaced as he sat down again. 'I hope she won't be disappointed when we meet. Did you find out when she's planning to come back to the UK?'

'Not for several more days, if Aunt Brenda has anything to do with it.'

'Splendid! That gives us time to fit in some of the trips I'd been thinking of, and spend some time with Dad as well. OK?'

'I'd like that,' Fleur said, her eyes bright.

He leaned across and took both her hands. 'And I like you,' he said in a deep, slow voice. 'Very much indeed.'

Fleur's inside fluttered wildly. All day, while they had been with Geoffrey at the villa, she had been wondering if she had dreamed the conversation of last night. Or if Eliot had regretted his hasty proposal and decided to accept her equally hasty refusal. In his father's presence he had been playful and teasing towards her. And when Geoffrey had disappeared to rest in his bedroom Eliot had settled himself in a corner of the veranda with a book and hardly seemed to notice she was there.

But now he was certainly noticing her. The lazy tone of his voice, the droop of dark lashes over glittering blue eyes, told her that there was much more he wanted to say—or do. His hands seemed to be urging her out of her chair, towards him. Oh, God, she thought, if he pulls me on to his knees I'm going to be lost. But how she wanted it! Wanted to nestle against him, her softness against his hard, strong body. Wanted to lift her mouth to his for a kiss that wouldn't be at all like the playful kisses he gave her when his father was present. She didn't know how she was going to last out a week without letting him know how much she wanted him. But somehow she had to try.

He said softly, 'Why don't you?'

'Why don't I what?' she said, looking down at his hands on hers.

'Why don't you do what comes naturally? What we both want?'

Very slowly she lifted her head and her eyes met his and she thought with a sudden shock of clear, certain knowledge that she loved him. It was like a flash of lightning that illuminated the whole room, making every part of it more sharply defined, more vividly coloured. It was too soon, almost unbelievable, but it had happened. She loved him and she wanted him, and the love and the wanting bore no resemblance at all to what she had felt for Roger. She loved Eliot, but she had to fight that love, because there was no future for her with him when only days ago he had been crazy for another girl. Later, perhaps, much later, if they were still seeing each other, perhaps—— She was hardly conscious of the muddled thoughts that were seething inside her head.

She was hardly conscious, either, of moving towards him, but there she was, on his knees, cradled in his arms, her head against his cheek, and it was—was simply the most wonderful sensation she had ever known.

He lifted her face, and his lips came down to hers and the sharp stab of erotic desire that spiralled through her shook her from head to foot like a fever. Her mouth moved against his as his kiss deepened. Her eyes closed as his hand came up to stroke her neck, found its way inside the low-cut bodice of her dress and moulded itself round her breast. She heard someone moaning and knew it was herself.

'Fleur——' His voice was low, close to her ear. 'Over there on the bed—couldn't we——?'

'No,' she gasped, and the word was dragged out of her. 'We can't—we mustn't. It's playing with fire—that's what you said.'

'I want you so badly,' he muttered, easing her on his knees so that she had no doubt that he was telling the truth. 'Please, darling. It's hell—and you want it too, don't you? Don't you?' he added raggedly. His face was so close to hers, she couldn't mistake the raw, hungry longing she saw there.

She struggled out of his arms and stood shivering as she looked down at him. 'Not when you're in love with Melissa. So soon afterwards—it would be—be disgusting.'

He laughed harshly. 'A man has needs that have nothing to do with what is known as love. Didn't anyone tell you that?'

His old patronising sneer again! She began to work herself up into a temper with him—it was the only defence she had. She lifted her chin. 'I'm not a child, of course I know that. But I'm still not willing to be used as a stand-in for another girl.' Her lip curled. 'Or should I say a lie-in?'

He was on his feet beside her now. 'Wasn't that rather a cheap gibe, Fleur?'

'Probably.' She shot the word at him icily. 'But I *am* only a girl from a flower shop. Had you forgotten?'

They stood glaring at each other like two animals preparing for fight. Eliot's eyes were cold as the sea, his mouth a hard, furious line, his fists clenched. Fleur's cheeks were flushed, her eyes glinting greenly.

Then, to her amazement, his face seemed to crumple up and he began to laugh. 'Oh, Fleur—darling little Fleur, what are we fighting about?' He went on laughing and she regarded him dubiously, trying to hang on to her trumped-up anger. But it was no use. A moment or two later she felt her mouth relax into a wry grin and then they were laughing together.

Fleur's emotions had been stirred painfully, and now her laughter verged on hysteria. She laughed until the tears ran down her cheeks and she didn't know whether she was laughing or crying. She staggered across to the bed and flopped down, and Eliot joined her, an arm holding her tightly. He gave her a handkerchief and she mopped her eyes. 'What a brute I am,' he declared. 'This isn't fair to you. When I suggested the plan, I didn't think far enough ahead. The whole situation has changed.'

'Has it?' Fleur questioned innocently, sniffing a little.

'You know damn well it has.'

She shook her head at him. 'I haven't changed,' she said, and thought, and may I be forgiven for that whopping lie!

'Of course you have, and so have I.' He sounded impatient now. 'They call it proximity,' he added.

Of *course*, she thought, in sudden disgust. Any pretty girl would have done as well for him at that moment. 'Sex, you mean?'

'Bright girl!'

Suddenly she was angry again, but coldly angry now. She stood up and made for the door. 'Well, we'll just have to deal with it, won't we? You know where I stand— I'm not going to be lured into your bed.'

He came after her and took her by both shoulders, looking down at her, and there was an odd expression in the blue eyes. 'But you do find me attractive, don't you, Fleur?' he said. 'Sexually attractive?' She was amazed by a note of—what was it?—entreaty almost in his voice.

'What a question!' she scoffed. 'You must have been assured of that more times than you can count—by more women.'

He shook her shoulders impatiently. 'Answer the question, Fleur. Do *you*?' There was a note of desperation in his voice.

They stared at each other in silence, and she felt a slow heat rising in her body. 'I—I——' she muttered. Her eyes lowered themselves to his mouth and she felt a spasm of desire, thrusting, pulsing. She wanted his mouth on her mouth—on her breast. She wanted it agonisingly. She wriggled violently in his grasp, pulling herself away.

Somehow, she managed a laugh. She supposed his male ego had been badly shaken by Melissa's defection, but it wasn't her job to build it up for him. 'I don't have to answer that; why should I? Sex doesn't enter into our agreement. I think I've convinced your father that I'm crazy about you, and you can't ask any more of me.' She went out and closed the door.

In her room, Fleur was in a thoroughly confused mood as she showered. She must have been out of her mind when the thought had struck her so suddenly that she was in love with Eliot. Of course it wasn't love, it was merely as the man said—proximity. She remembered what it had felt like when he had held her against him in the chair, and she shuddered as the cool water sluiced over her warm body. Yes, it was simply the old trap— sex. It complicated everything. For his father's sake she had to see this thing through for a few more days. After what had just happened, she didn't believe that Eliot would make any more passes at her. As for herself—she just had to ignore the voice inside that kept on telling her she was in love with him.

'I'm *not* in love with the man,' she said aloud. 'I'm not, I'm not.'

She went on saying it to herself as she stood in front of the polished dark-wood closet where her clothes hung. At the end of the rail, nearly out of sight, was the silvery chiffon dress with the pearl-trimmed shoulder straps. 'For when you both feel romantic,' Mandy had teased.

'Oh, no, Mandy,' Fleur murmured aloud. 'You got it all wrong.' She wouldn't be wearing that particular dress on *this* trip. She simply couldn't imagine, now, why she had allowed Mandy to persuade her to buy it. But it really was a heavenly dress! She sighed, touching the swirling folds of chiffon gently.

Stop it, she told herself, selecting a smart navy and white dress in a stiff silk. Don't start brooding about romance. Remember, you're not in love with the man. She repeated it to herself as she sat in front of her mirror doing her face with care and restraint, and fixing her tawny hair on top of her head with a white ribbon. She took a breath and muttered it as she went down to the bar to join Eliot for a pre-dinner drink.

She paused for a moment in the doorway, looking round, and when she saw him leaning on the bar her inside clenched painfully. She should be getting over it by now, she told herself, this overwhelming physical re-action to the sudden sight of him. He was chatting to a dark, wiry man whom Fleur now knew as Bruno, the owner of the hotel, and he was wearing a white jacket with a dark green shirt and trousers. He looked—superb. Both men were laughing and, in the brilliant light that played on the rows of bottles behind the bar, Eliot's teeth were dazzling white against the brown of his skin.

I'm not—*not* in love—— Fleur began a silent rep-etition that was almost a prayer. Then he turned and saw her and smiled, and her short revolt was over. It was like sinking into a warm sea as he came over and took her arm. 'Come and talk to Bruno,' he said. 'He says he hasn't had an opportunity of meeting my beautiful wife yet.'

As he led her across the room she could feel the
warmth of his arm through the thin stuff of his jacket.
She let herself lean a little towards him, and he looked
down and squeezed her arm. 'Friends?' he said softly.

'Friends,' she murmured. It wasn't enough—nowhere
near enough—but it would have to do.

Friends he had said and friends they remained during
the following days. Eliot had promised that she would
enjoy herself on this mock honeymoon, and he was certainly sparing no effort to that end. Each day he planned
something new.

'You're a historian,' he challenged her on Wednesday
morning. 'How's your Ligurian art history?'

Fleur pulled a rueful face. 'Pretty basic,' she admitted. 'I specialised in Northern European.'

'Right,' Eliot announced. 'We'll do a tourist flip along
the coast, then.'

The weather stayed good—warm and sunny, and each
day the white Ferrari sped along the sleek autostrada,
with its dizzying tunnels and viaducts, or drove more
sedately along the older road, the Via Aurelia, that
twisted and turned, following the coastline. And each
day there were a hundred new things for Fleur to marvel
at.

Most of the towns and villages they visited were new
to Eliot too, and it was exciting to discover fresh delights
together and to find out that their tastes often matched
each other—not always for the same reason. Fleur loved
the faded grandeur of the old quarters of the towns; the
somewhat shabby pilasters and porticos and window-
boxes; the tall houses squeezed together, their bright
paint of many years ago now mellowed to soft greens

and ochres and siennas. For his part, Eliot was fascinated by the architecture of the buildings as he and Fleur
wandered up and down the hilly streets of Genoa, gazing
at the baroque magnificence of one great *palazzo* after
another.

It was in Genoa that Eliot bought her an English
translation of a book telling the history of the great
seaport and its dramatic story from the fifth century BC
to the present day. 'For you to read in bed at night,' he
said, handing it over to her as they got back to the car.
'By the way, *do* you read in bed at night?' The blue eyes
danced wickedly.

'Always,' Fleur told him sedately, meeting the challenge without blinking. Eliot's approach to her had
changed, become more teasing and light-hearted. He had
evidently put aside his disappointment, and as each day
passed he became more and more delightful as a com-
panion. She liked listening to him talking about architecture, and he encouraged her to seek out the art
galleries that housed pictures by masters such as Titian,
Veronese and Van Dyck, as well as the less well-known
painters of Liguria. They saw the shimmering marble
quarries at Carrara, where Michelangelo chose his
massive blocks that were to be fashioned into the world's
greatest works of sculpture. They saw the grotto where
a tablet marked the famous swim of Lord Byron from
Portovenero to Lerici, over the Gulf of La Spezia. One
morning they visited the famous flower market off Piazza
Colombo in San Remo, and Fleur was in ecstasy over
the banks of marvellous colours and scents: tightly
budded roses and carnations, and exotic blooms that she
didn't even recognise, side by side with the more modest

offerings from the many flower farms which local growers had so ingeniously sited on the steep slopes of the area, where row upon row of glasshouses gleamed in the sunshine.

They took a boat trip along the coast of the Cinq Terre—five remote and starkly beautiful villages which seemed to be literally cut out of the jagged coastal rock, and above which vineyards rose, terraced at impossibly steep angles, and where a giant stone colossus stared down into the waves below.

They swam in the hotel pool and Fleur wore her 'tube', much to Eliot's amusement. They laughed a lot and teased each other like children. And when they were tired of sightseeing Eliot drove up into the mountains and they discovered tiny hidden villages where they could eat a simple lunch and doze away the siesta-time afterwards under the pine trees. And even when they lay under the trees he made no attempt to touch her or turn the occasion into a flirtation, mild or otherwise. By degrees Fleur concluded that she had been mistaken in thinking he intended to use her as a substitute for his lost love. Or, if he had, he had decided to give up the attempt. She tried to convince herself that she was glad.

After every expedition they returned to the villa to spend the evening with Eliot's father and tell him of their day's adventures. It seemed to Fleur that each day Geoffrey grew stronger and more lively. By the end of the week he was walking without the aid of a stick, and pacing up and down the terrace with Fleur beside him as they watched Eliot below, making an effort to finish putting the rocky garden into shape before they left.

'So you're going back to England tomorrow, Fleur?' Geoffrey sighed. 'I shall miss you both terribly. This time has been a life-saver for me—literally, I mean. D'you know, my dear child——' he sat down on a cane seat and she sat beside him '—I feel quite different, as if I'd been granted a new lease of life. I'd really begun to believe that I'd come to the end. I suppose the psychologists are right, and that's what happiness can do for you.'

'I'm so glad,' Fleur told him, sincerity shining out of clear green eyes. 'It's wonderful, and you're looking so much better, too.' It was true. He no longer looked like an ailing, elderly man. There was colour in his cheeks and some of the lines had smoothed out of his face, leaving only the ones that give interest and dignity to an older man. Even the grey hair, with its streaks of white, seemed crisper. He was a very handsome man, Fleur thought, although she could hardly tell him that. Instead, she smiled into the blue eyes that were so like Eliot's. 'I'm very, very glad,' she said again.

'And what's such a comfort to me,' Geoffrey went on, 'is to know that Eliot has found a wife in a million—a lovely, warm girl who will be a real wife to him.' He paused. 'I don't want to sound fulsome and embarrass you, Fleur, but I have to tell you that you're a great joy to me. I was so——' he hesitated again '—so afraid that my son might make a terrible mistake, as I did myself. I expect you've gathered that already?'

'Yes,' Fleur murmured. She felt dreadful. If she had committed some crime, she couldn't have felt worse. What had she done? What had both she and Eliot done, in deceiving his father as they had? She almost burst into tears. Instead she touched Geoffrey's hand, and he looked at her and smiled and put an arm affectionately round her waist, drawing her nearer.

Eliot came climbing up the steeply sloping garden towards them, threading his way between the rocks and the sprawling plants that half covered them. It was a hot day and he was wearing only denim shorts and he looked magnificent, Fleur thought, as the late afternoon sun shone through the leaves of the vine overhanging the terrace on to bronzed skin and rippling muscles.

He flopped down on the cool marble floor of the terrace, stretching out luxuriously. 'Phew, I'm creased! It's too hot for this game.' Eliot grinned up at the two on the garden seat, staring pointedly at the way that Geoffrey's arm was around Fleur's waist. 'Hey, Dad, what are you up to? She's *my* wife, remember?'

So natural, the easy, teasing companionship. Fleur could hardly bear it. 'I'll get you a long, cold drink, darling,' she said, getting up quickly. 'You look as if you could do with it.' And she escaped to the kitchen, where Luisa was preparing lunch.

When she returned, with a tray of tall, frosted glasses filled with the tangy fruit drink that was Luisa's 'special', the two men were discussing a plan for the next day.

'I thought,' Eliot told Fleur, 'that as it's going to be our last day here we might all go along to the Hanbury Gardens at La Mortola. Dad can take it very easily and just do as much walking as he feels like. What do you think?'

'Oh, yes, that would be lovely,' she agreed quickly. Anything—anywhere—just so long as she and Eliot

wouldn't have to be alone together as the strange bitter-
sweet week of the 'honeymoon' came to an end.

Geoffrey looked doubtfully from one to the other of
them. 'You're sure? It seems a shame to spend the last
bit of your honeymoon with a crock of an ancient parent,
and I shan't be able to walk very far, I'm afraid.' He
shook his head in amazement. 'It's a miracle that I feel
able to walk at all. I'd given up hope of ever seeing my
lovely Gardens again. It's so very good of you two
children to give me the chance.'

Eliot took the glass that Fleur handed him and reached
up to encircle her slim waist. 'We want to, don't we,
sweetheart?' His eyes were very blue and—she almost
hated him for the way he could put on an act—very
tender, as he said, 'We've got the rest of our lives
together, so what's one morning?'

But once they had said goodnight to Geoffrey, after
dining at the villa for their last evening, and left for the
drive back to San Remo, the tenderness was gone. Eliot
was terse and businesslike as he left her at the door of
her room, saying, 'You may as well get packed tonight,
Fleur, and we'll check out after breakfast. We'll take
Dad to the Gardens in the morning, have a quick lunch
with him and then be on our way. We've got a lot of
miles to cover.'

Fleur opened her eyes wide. 'We're driving home?'

'Well, what do you think?' he said impatiently as they
stood together at the door of her bedroom. 'I haven't
bought the car in order to leave it behind.' He wasn't in
the best of moods tonight, she could see that. Probably
he was not liking the idea of leaving his father alone
again.

'I'm sorry,' she said rather helplessly. 'I hadn't thought about it.'

'Well, think now,' he said in his most disagreeable tone. 'We'll meet at breakfast. Goodnight, Fleur.' He opened the door for her, and she went in and closed it promptly. All right, she thought mutinously, *be* like that if you want to. What did it matter now? The charade was almost over.

Fleur slept badly that night and was up early, finishing the last of her packing. She laid the silvery chiffon dress, carefully wrapped in its tissue, on top of the larger of her two cases. 'Poor thing—— she touched it lovingly '—you deserved a better fate than to be left hanging in the dark all week. No romantic evenings for you!' She smiled to herself at the foolishness of talking to a dress, but her eyes were moist. She recognised that she was in an emotional state this morning and she had to snap out of it. The end of anything was always a bit sad, she thought, and it had been a good week in a strange kind of way. Satisfactory, because Geoffrey seemed to have a new lease of life, and sad, because after today she wasn't going to see him again. She had grown very fond of Eliot's father in these few days, and he made no secret that he had grown fond of her.

Some day Eliot was going to have to confess to his father about the trick they had played on him. Or would he try to continue the deception, in letters, in phone calls, referring to Fleur, talking about her? Surely he couldn't keep that up for long? But how would Geoffrey react to the news that he had been duped—for that was what it amounted to? She didn't dare to imagine. Eliot would no doubt manage to explain it all, but even so Geoffrey would surely be hurt and bewildered.

Fleur shook her head, as if she could shake away the thoughts that nagged at her. The important thing was to make this last morning together a happy time for Geoffrey, and she was going to do her very best to see that it was.

And it *was* a happy time. Geoffrey was thrilled to see his beloved Gardens again, and his pleasure spilled over to the other two. If Eliot was feeling guilt at his duplicity, he certainly didn't show it.

Fleur didn't have to pretend to enjoy their visit to the famous Gardens. Geoffrey knew all the history of the place, and the names of the rare plants brought here from all over the world, and she plied him with questions as they strolled along, stopping frequently as Geoffrey recognised an old favourite in an exotic flower or a shrub with long, sword-sharp leaves that made Fleur shudder. Splashes of cream and gold and crimson lay like small lakes against the dark green of the foliage; great bell-like blooms hung on the ends of delicately-drooping stems.

'Oh, how my mother would adore all this!' Fleur burst out, as they paused on a white marble terrace, leaning on the balustrade to look down over the tops of the acres of lushly growing things to where the blue of the Mediterranean showed between the tops of the palm trees.

Eliot turned his back to the view, looking lazily at Fleur. 'Nothing easier,' he said. 'We'll bring her down very soon for a visit. We could spend Christmas here. It wouldn't be too late to see the Gardens. It's the most extraordinary quirk of the climate—they have over a thousand flowers in bloom on New Year's Day, isn't that so, Dad?'

Fleur didn't hear Geoffrey's reply. So Eliot was keeping up the charade until the very last moment, was he? He was raising his father's hopes still further—for Geoffrey would be delighted to meet a fellow enthusiast and show her all his precious flowers. He would look forward to it when they had left him alone again—and then he would be horribly let down and disappointed when he knew the truth. Angry tears gathered behind Fleur's eyelids and she blinked them away. She glanced up at Eliot's smiling face. Oh, how could he? How could he?

Lunch, back at the villa, was rather an anticlimax. Eliot couldn't hide his anxiety to be away, and Geoffrey was obviously doing his best to keep up his spirits until they had left. Fleur carried the coffee-tray out to Luisa in the kitchen and left the two men together.

'I am so sorry you go,' Luisa shrugged eloquently. 'Signor Stevens so *contento*—so 'appy—while you are here. I cannot believe.' She heaved a deep sigh. 'Before you come I am afraid——' She shook her head dolefully, launching into Italian, the gist of which was only too clear to Fleur. Luisa had not expected Geoffrey to live very long. Then she cheered up. 'But you come with your 'usband and then Signor Stevens——' She snapped her fingers in the air. 'Sudden, 'e well. *Meglio*. You come back very soon, *si*?'

'Very soon.' Fleur hated this business of lying, and disappointing people she liked.

She hated even more having to smile and make the same promises when they said goodbye to Geoffrey. As the Ferrari passed along the short gravelled drive she turned back to wave, and saw him standing, a solitary figure, an arm raised in salute. Her throat choked up and she burrowed down into her seat, feeling utterly wretched.

At another time Fleur would have relished the drive north, through the most spectacular scenery she had ever seen. The Ferrari purred effortlessly up into the mountains, where the white peaks of the Alps soared into the blue sky, through the gloomy tunnels of the pass and slowly down again. Trees replaced rocks beside the motorway, the landscape became more gentle as they crossed the border.

Eliot drove in silence as the hours passed, and Fleur, stealing a glance now and then at his stern profile, wondered what was going on in that part of his mind that wasn't concerned with driving. None of his thoughts could be very happy, she guessed. His plan to pass her off as his wife had succeeded as well—better, perhaps—than he could have hoped. But he must surely now be feeling miserably guilty, as she was. She had a sudden overwhelming impulse to touch him, to let him know that she understood. How soppy can you get? she thought bitterly. Eliot wouldn't welcome her understanding: he had told her so in no uncertain terms not so long ago. She closed her eyes as the car sped onwards and the sun set in gaudy streaks of gold and green in the western sky, and eventually she dropped off into a light sleep. Dreams came and went, dreams of Eliot, erotic half-dreams that wakened her, flushed and trembling, only to drift away again as the steady throb of the engine lulled her into more dreaming...

'Are you asleep, Fleur?'

She opened her eyes, to find that the car had stopped. 'W-where are we?' she asked muzzily. The lights of what looked like a hotel gleamed into the darkness.

'Within sight and smell of food,' Eliot said. 'This is where we eat. Come along.'

He came round and opened the door on her side. Fleur blinked, trying to gather her wits together. 'Ooh, I'm stiff with sitting so long.' She half fell out of the car, and Eliot was there to put his arm round her. It felt strong and somehow—right, and she resisted the urge to pull away as he drew her close against him. He didn't have to do that now—there was nobody here to convince that they were lovers. The sooner she got used to that dreary fact, the better, she told herself, making a tardy effort to release herself.

It didn't work. In the near-darkness he merely put the other arm round her. 'Darling little Fleur,' he murmured against her cheek. 'I've been watching you sleep. It's put all sorts of ideas into my head.'

She felt a blush begin somewhere in the middle of her body and spread outward. 'I—I thought you said you were hungry,' she murmured.

'I am. I'm hungry for you, my darling, ravenously hungry.'

There was a thick, urgent note in his voice, and she felt an answering urgency inside herself. When his mouth came down to hers she could make no pretence of re-sisting. As his tongue prised her lips open she answered his kiss with a passion as strong as his own. They clung together, bodies locked, their lips, tongues, loving each other wildly. Dimly Fleur realised that this hunger was the pay-off for their play-acting at love all this last week. They had played with fire once too often, and now the sudden blaze was burning them up. At last he let her go, but only far enough to whisper urgently, 'Fleur—this is where I planned to stay. There's a room booked—only one room. Shall we share it?'

She didn't have to think—anyway, she wasn't capable of thought. 'Yes,' she said. 'Oh, yes,' and heard his harsh intake of breath as he led her towards the open entrance door of the hotel.

Fleur was hardly conscious of the surroundings as she stood waiting while Eliot checked in at the reception counter. She had a vague impression that the hotel was small—a country hotel, somewhere in France. She didn't know where they were, nor did she care. All she was conscious of was the swelling, urgent need of her body as she stood watching Eliot's tall, strong back. Oh, God, she loved him, loved him. She'd never dreamed there could be loving and wanting like this.

A boy in uniform went before them up the stairs, carrying their bags, and opened a door at the end of a short corridor. *'Merci, m'sieur.'* He grinned widely and departed with his tip.

The room was large and comfortably furnished—that was the impression Fleur got. All she had time to get, for as she met Eliot's gaze, fixed on her, moving over her body as she pulled off the light coat that covered her cotton dress, she had one thought and one only. One pulsating, overpowering desire—to give to him all he needed from her. With shaking hands she pulled down the zip of her dress and let it slide to the floor. Shameless, that's what I am, shameless, she thought, and gloried in the word.

He stood very still while she unfastened her bra with shaking fingers and then wriggled out of her lacy panties and stood before him naked, her bright hair curling round her flushed cheeks.

'Oh, dear God—incredible——' she heard him mutter. And then, at last, she felt his hands at her waist, drawing her against him, moving over her warm, smooth skin.

The bed was soft and cool. The duvet was pushed aside and Fleur lay waiting while Eliot shed his shirt and trousers. Then he was beside her, resting on his elbows, looking down at her in the concealed light that threw dark shadows over the room.

'You're so beautiful, so very beautiful,' he muttered. 'Have you any idea what it's cost me, this last week, to control myself—to say goodnight at the door of your bedroom? To play at being lovers for Dad's benefit, when every time I came near you I wanted to carry you off and lay you on a bed—like this—and touch you— like this—and this——' His hands moved over her, stroking, pressing, seeking the most erotic places until she was nearly screaming with her need. Her arms twined round his neck, drawing him closer, then slid down his body to his hips, inviting, enticing.

He needed no enticing. There was nothing gentle in his kisses, they were almost anguished as his mouth moved to her breast, fastening on the hard, peaked nipples, his tongue caressing them until she cried out with the tumult that was rising inside her.

His passion was raging like a white-hot furnace now; he was trembling violently against her and she could only

guess at all the frustration and unsatisfied desire that
was working in him, fuelling his need.

'Darling—darling——' she moaned, responding to
him with a violence equal to his own. She knew now
that she had wanted this ever since the first moment she
saw him, towering over her in the dark passage by the
quay. All that resentment, all that anger and indignation
had been building up into the explosive force that was
finding its way out in his arms.

His hand was on her thigh, stroking urgently, moving
upwards until it found the place it was seeking, and he
cried out in triumph, sliding his body down against her
until she felt the hard thrust of him above her, inside
her, and gave herself up to a wild, plunging ecstasy that
rocked them both with a tumult of primitive desire until
they reached a climax that went on and on, shuddering
sweet, and died away slowly into a relaxation so complete that her limbs were weightless, floating in a warm
sea of fulfilment.

Eliot rolled away and lay still, his harsh breathing
slowly returning to normal. Then one arm went round
her, moulding her into the curve of his body. 'Dear little
Fleur,' he murmured in her ear. 'I needed that so much.
Dear—sweet—Fleur——' The words died away on a
deep sigh and she knew that he was asleep.

Fleur didn't sleep. She lay in Eliot's arms and her
thoughts and feelings began to skitter round until she
didn't know which was which. She should have been
blissfully contented. She had just made love with the
man she loved. But instead she felt a black depression
creeping up on her. She was deeply, painfully in love
with Eliot, and their lovemaking had shown her that he

was the only one—there wasn't going to be another man in her life for years, perhaps for ever. She knew with a horrid clarity that that was the truth, even though it wasn't very sensible or reasonable. But he didn't love her, and nothing less would do.

I needed that so much, he had said. She had helped him over a bad patch, but a man's need was easily aroused, quickly forgotten when it was satisfied. There was only one course for her, she decided bleakly, and that was to get out of his life as soon as she could.

Beside her, Eliot stirred and turned towards her, smiling sleepily. 'God, I feel wonderful,' he breathed. Then an odd look came into his face. 'Fleur, I should have asked you before only I got rather carried away. You weren't—at risk—were you?'

A faint smile touched her lips, a smile that was more than a little cynical. 'As it happens, no, I wasn't.'

His sigh of relief hurt her. But his next words sent her emotions reeling.

'Good,' he said. 'It's much better to plan things. But it wouldn't have mattered all that much, because you *are* going to marry me, aren't you?'

Fleur shot up in bed and sat leaning against the quilted back-rest, green eyes sparking. 'We've been here before, I seem to remember. I said no then and I'm saying no again. You've got a devious way of getting what you think you want, Mr Stevens.'

'Oh, darling Fleur, shut up and come back and listen to me.' He reached up lazily and grabbed her arm, pulling her down beside him. She kept her face stiffly averted as he went on, 'You can't really believe that all—this——' the arm that wasn't holding her waved towards the rumpled bedclothes '—was a put-up job to get my own way.'

His hand came up to her chin and turned her face round.

'Look at me, Fleur, and tell me you can't.'

The blue eyes were gazing steadily into hers. She said reluctantly, 'Oh, well, I suppose you didn't plan it. It just worked out rather conveniently for you.'

He chuckled, deep in his throat. 'Convenient wouldn't be the word I'd choose, but let it go. Did it work out— *conveniently*—for you too, my dear little Fleur? Did you enjoy it?'

She felt a stupid blush rising and her whole body was warm and languid again, but she thrust the feeling away. 'You know I did,' she said crossly. 'You're an expert at the game, you know how to turn a girl on—you must have had plenty of practice. As I told you before, sex without love doesn't make a good marriage.'

'It makes a damn good start,' he told her. 'You have to trust that the loving will come later.' He lifted himself up and rested on one elbow, looking down into her face. 'I truly believe that with us it would. I think we could make a good marriage, I like you enormously, Fleur. And there's something else, something I haven't told you.'

'Yes?' she said cautiously. What was his game now?

'Just before we left, Dad told me that he had decided to come back to England. He said he wanted to use the time he had left, not mope it away feeling sorry for himself. He said that seeing us together had given him something to live for, and certainly he seems a different man. He's been making all sorts of plans—he wants to meet your mother, Fleur, and possibly back her in her florist's business. Maybe even open new shops.' He paused, looking hard at her. 'So you see——?'

Oh, yes, she saw. She saw all the reasons why Eliot wanted to marry her. They were such persuasive reasons—only one reason was missing. The most important one of all. He couldn't honestly tell her that he loved her.

And she would rather die than admit that she loved him.

CHAPTER EIGHT

FLEUR slid out of bed and picked up her clothes from the floor. She didn't look at Eliot, although she was tinglingly aware that he was watching her every movement.

'I suppose there's a shower about here somewhere?' she said, trying to sound nonchalant.

'Bound to be.' Eliot heaved himself from the bed with a grunt and started to explore the room. Fleur couldn't help stealing a glance at him. In the dim light he looked magnificent naked, his body firm and glistening, like an athlete's body. Her heart began to behave erratically.

'Oops!' he chuckled, opening the door on to the corridor by mistake. 'No, this must be the one, over here. In you go, love. Shall I come and help you?'

'No,' squealed Fleur, disappearing into the shower-room and locking the door quickly. She could guess what would happen if they shared the shower, and she needed these few minutes alone—to think.

But when she was standing under the jets of warm water thinking proved difficult. She soaped herself dreamily, remembering—remembering——

Oh, snap out of it, she told herself and turned the tap to cold, gasping with shock as the icy water struck her skin. It must come straight off the Alps, she thought, as she leapt out of the shower and started to towel down vigorously. But it did the trick. Her reasoning brain was working again, she assured herself.

To accept Eliot's proposal or not? It was a straight choice, and she tried to line up the pros and cons. There was really only one con—that he didn't love her. You have to trust that the loving will come later, he had said. She put on panties and bra and slipped into the cream jersey dress she had been wearing to travel in. She inspected herself in the full-length mirror on the wall. Her hair was wildly dishevelled, her cheeks were pink and her eyes were shining. Her mouth twitched at the corners. 'Look at you,' she said aloud, 'you don't need to reason it all out, do you? If you refuse, you'll never make love with Eliot again. So that's it, decision made.'

When she went back into the bedroom Eliot was kneeling on the floor in front of his open travel bag. He'd pulled on a pair of striped trunks and he looked around at her and grinned. 'I've made myself decent, you see.'

'*I'm* not decent, my hair's an absolute bird's nest.' She ran her fingers through the tumble of tawny curls. 'Has my small dressing-case come up—I need a brush and a comb—oh, and some make-up if we're dining here——' she chattered on. Suddenly she was overcome with shyness.

Eliot got to his feet. He came over and stood before her, touching her bright hair gently. 'It looks great,' he said. 'It looks as if you've just made love.' His eyes were steady as he said quietly, 'Well—what's the answer, Fleur? Have you decided?'

It wasn't easy to meet that deep blue gaze and tell him only half the truth, but it had to be done. 'I've thought of all the—the circumstances——' she said. 'And I've decided that this is one risk I'm willing to take. It—it's mostly because of your father, Eliot. I hated leaving him like that. I hated having to lie to him, and if he's coming back to England he would find out and he'd be hurt badly to know we'd tricked him——' Her lips trembled. 'So—yes, I'll marry you, Eliot, as soon as you like.'

She heard his quick intake of breath, and one arm went round her in what seemed to her like a triumphant hug. 'Thank you, my dear. I promise I won't let you down.'

He stretched out his other arm and consulted his watch. 'Ten to eight,' he said. 'It'll be early afternoon in Miami. I suggest we phone your mother and tell her the news. We can find out when she's coming back, and then we can arrange to get married in London as soon as she arrives.'

His tone was so businesslike that Fleur felt a chill of foreboding. Was this what marriage to Eliot was going to be like—he making the decisions, giving the orders, she obeying? As he crossed the room to the bedside phone, she said in a small voice, 'You're very clever at getting your own way, aren't you, Eliot?'

He turned, surprised, dark brows raised. 'Not always,' he said. And she knew, with a sinking heart, that he was thinking of Melissa.

Aunt Brenda answered the phone. 'Fleur—great to hear you. Your mother's out shopping—I had to wait in for the man to fix a faucet. I guess she's buying a gift to bring home to you. We planned to contact you when she came back to tell you she's flying home tomorrow. Arriving at Heathrow—oh, goodness, I forget the time.

But never mind—she's aiming to get back home to Cornwall by train, I do know that. Now, how are you, Fleur dear? And how is your great adventure proceeding?'

'I'm fine,' Fleur said. 'We're on our way home too, driving in Eliot's new car. A Ferrari—how about that?'

She heard Aunt Brenda's wolf-whistle. 'Honey— you've sure got yourself an impressive guy!'

'Haven't I just?' This was stupid, wasting a call being jokey with Aunt Brenda, but no way was Fleur going to let her mother get the news secondhand. 'Must go now, Auntie dear,' she added quickly. 'I just wanted Mum to know I'm on my way back to London and I'll be seeing her very soon.' A few more loving messages, and she replaced the phone on its cradle.

She turned to Eliot, who was emerging from the shower-room, fully dressed. 'My mother wasn't there, but Aunt Brenda says she's flying to Heathrow tomorrow, and then going on to Cornwall by train.'

He nodded. 'Our news will have to keep, then. We might try to contact her at the airport. If not, we'll persuade her to come back to London for the wedding.'

Without thinking, Fleur began, 'Why couldn't we——?'

'Get married in Porthgurran?' Eliot's face was a closed mask. 'Oh, no, that wouldn't do at all.' He turned away abruptly. 'Now, will you get packed while I shower? We can take the bags with us when we go down for dinner.'

It would have been reassuring if Eliot had decided to stay overnight at the pleasant, small hotel where they had dinner. It would have been much more than reassuring, it would have been heaven to have shared the wide bed with him all through the night. Fleur ached to have his arms hold her again; every time she looked at him across the white-clothed dinner-table with its posy of tiny rosebuds, her pulses set up an urgent throb and her inside felt hollow with desire. But it was all too evident that Eliot had other ideas. Having worn down her resistance and assuaged his immediate sexual needs, he was now keen to move on to the next item on the agenda. He had stacked their cases into the car before they even started dinner.

He didn't linger over coffee. 'Finished, Fleur? We'll get along, then. We should make good time for Boulogne now; we'll catch an early ferry and be in London before lunch. There'll be time for me to go along to the office to check on things there. That OK with you? You can have a good sleep in the car.'

Well, at least he had consulted her wishes—albeit somewhat late and somewhat briefly. 'What about you?' she said. 'Are you going to drive all night without sleep?'

'Nothing new, I often do,' he said casually. 'And I'm on a high at the moment.' Suddenly the blue eyes blazed into hers with unmistakable meaning. 'Guess why?'

Meeting that blatantly sexy look, Fleur almost began to plead with him to stay overnight. But already he was on his feet, asking for his bill to be prepared. As the smiling waiter helped her on with her coat, she sighed and accepted the inevitable fact that she was only a very small part of Eliot's life, whereas he seemed to be the whole of hers.

Fleur had almost forgotten what the flat in Chelsea looked like. So much had happened since she first came here just over a week ago that it was like stepping into a new world. It was really a beautiful room, she thought, walking over to the long windows to look out at the view across the Thames. She tried to imagine herself living here, married to Eliot, but she couldn't.

She wandered into the kitchen, where Eliot had gone to put the coffee percolator on. 'Shall we be living here when——' she hesitated '—when we're married?'

'Hm? Oh, yes, for the moment. I'll have to look for somewhere larger later on, I suppose.' He didn't sound very interested.

Fleur wandered back into the living-room and sat down, feeling chilled. She needed his reassurance, not the rather abrupt, taking-her-for-granted way he had treated her since she had promised to marry him. She wanted—oh, above everything she wanted to hear him say he loved her. That would make everything right— only it wasn't going to happen.

'Coffee up,' Eliot announced, carrying in a tray. 'This will keep me awake for another hour or two. I'll get along to the office now—they'll be expecting me. And I can't leave the car outside any longer or I'll be nabbed. Will you phone Heathrow and try to find out a likely flight that your mother might be on?'

He tossed down a mug of black coffee and had poured out a second one when the entry-phone buzzed. Taking his mug with him, he strode across the room. 'Who the hell's this likely to be?' he muttered, and pressed a lever. 'Yes?'

There was a silence, and he clicked his tongue impatiently and began to turn away. Then a girl's voice quavered, 'Eliot——'

'Melissa!' The mug of coffee jerked in his hand and the dark liquid ran down on to the pale carpet. His voice was suddenly flat, the colour had drained out of his face, leaving it ashen under his tan.

'Eliot, can I come up—I must speak to you—please——' The words trailed away into a sob.

He turned his head and looked straight at Fleur, who hadn't moved from her chair. He said curtly, 'No, you can't come up, Melissa. Stay there and I'll come down to you.'

Fleur got stiffly to her feet. 'I could go—somewhere—out—if you like,' she muttered, but he broke in abruptly,

'No, you stay here, I'll have to go down and sort this out. Bear with me, Fleur, just give me a little while. Don't go away, will you? Promise?'

He looked—distraught. She hadn't seen him look like that before, not even after the traumatic events at the church. He hesitated for a split second, as if there were something he needed to say to her, but then he turned away and went quickly out of the flat.

Fleur walked to the window on leaden feet. She knew now that she had always, at the back of her mind, expected this to happen. Whatever the reason for Melissa's non-appearance at her wedding, she would come back and explain it and beg Eliot to forgive her—and he would. Of course he would. If you love someone, you forgive them, that's one of the things about loving, Fleur thought dully. That's the way it works.

She pulled open the long window and stepped out on to the narrow wrought-iron balcony, wondering briefly if it were safe or if she would come crashing down at

Eliot's feet. She smiled wryly. At this moment, it didn't seem to matter very much.

But the balcony received her weight without a grumble. She took a long breath of air from the river, mixed with the usual addition of exhaust fumes from the ceaseless traffic passing along the Embankment. The white Ferrari stood outside the big front door, and as she stared down Eliot appeared, with Melissa beside him. She wore a white suit and her silver-gilt hair hung loosely into her neck. From this angle Fleur could see nothing of her face, until, for a moment, she raised her head and looked up at Eliot, and even from a distance her beauty shone out, fair and exquisitely delicate. She said something and he pulled a handkerchief out and wiped her eyes gently, one arm protectively round her slim shoulders. Then he unlocked the car door and handed her in as if she were infinitely precious. A moment later he was behind the wheel and the powerful car was moving away from the kerb to join the queue of cars heading for Westminster.

Fleur went inside again and closed the window very quietly. Well, that's that, she thought, the end of something that had hardly begun. It had been such a pathetic little episode, falling in love with a man who was merely using her and made no secret of the fact. If she could have blamed him, if she could have accused him or been madly angry, it might have helped, but he hadn't lied to her or led her to expect anything but a marriage of— well, not of convenience, but of friendship. He wanted a wife to make the warm, happy home he had never known. He wanted her, particularly, because she had endeared herself to his father. He wanted a girl in his bed——

Automatically she went into the kitchen and found a damp cloth to wipe up the coffee stain from the carpet. She rubbed and rubbed, but the stain refused obstinately to be removed, and after a time she found that her tears were dropping on to it, but even that didn't make any difference. Somehow it seemed the last straw. She covered her face with her hands and sank back on her knees and wept great choking sobs.

A long time later she dragged herself into the bathroom and bathed her face. She found her small travelling-case and sat down before the dressing-table mirror and tried to disguise her swollen eyelids and flushed cheeks. The charade wasn't quite over yet. She had to play her part to the end, and the fact that she had fallen in love with him wasn't included in her role.

Don't go away, he'd said, and she wouldn't. She would see the thing through with—well, it sounded corny, but it was all she had left—with dignity. She had seen the way he looked at her, frowning, after Melissa's message—as if she were some embarrassing encumbrance that he didn't quite know how to get rid of without having to think too badly of himself.

She didn't think he would bring Melissa back here. She would be kept in the wings, ready to move in when Fleur had been disposed of. He would be tactful, regretful. He would remind her kindly and gently that she'd known the score from the start. He would probably thank her again for helping him out with the problem of his father's disappointment.

'You do understand, don't you, Fleur?' he might even plead with her. She would be very kind, very calm. She would assure him that Geoffrey would surely forgive the deception and accept the real Melissa just as he had accepted her. Oh, yes, she would be very reasonable. At least he would admire her composure.

She outlined her lips carefully. Don't be idiotic, of course he won't, she told her reflection. He won't be thinking of you at all, except how to get rid of you gracefully. That thought made her want to weep again, but she clenched her nails into her palms and squeezed her eyelids together until the spasm passed. Then, without even a glance at the wide bed that she had slept on that first night, when it had all begun, she went back to the corner of the sofa in the living-room, picked up a motoring magazine from the coffee-table and leafed through the pages of glossy sleek monsters without seeing a thing.

Ring up Heathrow and try to find out what time your mother's flight might arrive, Eliot had suggested. But there was no point in doing that now. Even if she could trace a possible flight, she didn't know how she would get from Chelsea to Heathrow. She had only the cash that had been in her handbag when she had left Porthgurran, and she hadn't needed any since. It certainly wasn't enough to pay for a taxi to Heathrow, even if she could find one. Besides, she didn't feel equal to facing Janet—not yet. She would see her soon, and by then she might have risen above the desolation that had her in its grip. What a blessing, she thought wearily, that her mother had been out when she'd phoned last night. If she'd blurted it all out about getting married, that would have complicated things even further.

The minutes crawled by and turned into hours. What was Eliot doing? Surely it wouldn't take him all this time to comfort Melissa, perhaps leave her at some nearby hotel to wait until the flat was clear for her to move in?

It would be nearly rush-hour time in the city. She wondered if he had called in at his office before returning, taking Melissa with him. Oh, God, why didn't he come? Why did she have to wait so long to get this last painful scene acted out, so that the final curtain could come down?

She got up and paced round the room. It was getting cold in the flat now. Eliot hadn't switched on the heating and she didn't know how to do it. Suddenly she realised that she had had nothing to eat since dinner last night, but the thought of food made her feel sick. Tea, though, would be comforting. There was nothing like a cup of tea when you were feeling bad—such as when your heart was breaking into little pieces, she thought, with a feeble attempt to see some humour in the situation.

In the luxury kitchen she put the kettle on to boil, chose a Darjeeling tin from the selection of tins of tea, set cup and saucer on a tray and found milk in the fridge. All very slowly and deliberately. All taking up as much time as possible.

She drank two cups of tea. Surely Eliot would be back soon? She was aware that her forehead was clammy damp, in spite of the chill of the atmosphere. If there had been a car crash—how would she know? His address would be in his pocket book—the hospital would phone. She walked across to the desk and looked at the telephone as if she could will it to ring, to relieve the oppressive silence that surrounded her like a fog. Even the noise of traffic hardly penetrated through the double-glazing of the big windows.

Then she saw that the receiver had been knocked sideways off its cradle, so that it was half hanging, not making a proper connection. The cleaning woman was probably responsible for that, when she was dusting.

Fleur's inside went hollow. There *had* been a car crash—she was sure of it. And if the phone wasn't working the hospital couldn't get into contact. They would send a policeman—Janet had said that was how she had heard about Tom's fatal accident. Two policemen had called. They were so kind, so sympathetic, she said—— Fleur closed her eyes to blot out the harrowing pictures that arose in her mind.

There was the sound of a door opening. Eliot's voice called, 'Fleur—I'm back, and look who I've brought with me.'

Fleur spun round. Thank God—he was alive, he hadn't had a crash. It didn't even seem to matter that he had Melissa with him.

The door of the living-room opened and he stood there, smiling. And by his side, smiling even more widely, holding out her arms and wearing a new tweed coat, stood Janet.

Fleur stared glassily at the two of them. 'What——' she croaked. And then her legs went from under her and she fell backwards on to the sofa as the room began to revolve slowly before her eyes.

It wasn't much of a faint. Eliot was pushing her head down between her knees and Janet was sitting beside her, smoothing back her hair, crooning anxiously, 'Poor sweet, it was a shock, seeing me walk in like that.'

Fleur sat up shakily and found herself being hugged and held close while Eliot disappeared and came back holding a glass. He sank down on his knees and held the glass to her lips. 'Drink up,' he ordered, and Fleur obeyed, coughing as the fiery liquid burnt her throat.

'The child's probably starving with hunger.' He seemed to be addressing Janet. Then Fleur felt his hand on her shoulder, warm and blissfully reassuring, although why it should be reassuring she couldn't make out. 'Have you had anything to eat since I left, Fleur? No, you haven't. And what's happened to the phone? I've been trying to get through to you on and off for hours.'

Fleur blinked at him. 'It was—was pushed off the cradle thing, I just found it,' she muttered and grinned foolishly. 'I don't think much of your Mrs Mop's dusting.'

Eliot groaned. 'Oh lor', yes. She's done that before. Well, never mind that now, sweetheart. As soon as you feel up to it we're going to Mario's to have a meal. A celebration meal—just for the three of us.'

He was calling her 'sweetheart'. He had somehow brought her mother with him. And what were they supposed to be celebrating? It didn't make much sense.

Janet said, 'If we're going out to eat, may I tidy myself up somewhere?' With a loving smile towards Fleur, she took her small travelling-case and disappeared through the doorway that Eliot pointed out to her.

He came back and sat next to Fleur on the sofa. 'Are you really feeling better, love?' He put an arm gently round her and drew her close.

It was wonderful to feel cherished. She allowed herself the luxury of laying her head against his shoulder. 'Oh, yes, I'm fine now. I suppose I was hungry.'

'Mario will soon remedy that. If we go now there won't be too many people there; we might even have the place to ourselves.' He rubbed his cheek against the top of her head. 'You gave me a shock when you flaked out like that.'

'I don't know what happened,' she said weakly. 'I don't make a habit of it. I'd been sitting here waiting for ages, and I thought——' she swallowed '—I began to have all sorts of awful thoughts about a car crash. And then—when you came back I thought it was Melissa you had brought with you.'

The pressure of his cheek on her head increased, his arm drew her closer. 'And you supposed that Melissa and I had had a grand reconciliation, that all was forgiven and that I was about to suggest to you that in the circumstances you and I might forgo our—er—arrangement.'

'Something like that,' she mumbled.

He drew away a little and lifted her face so that he could look into her eyes as he said in an odd voice, 'You were quite wrong. But would it have mattered to you all that much if you had been right?'

She studied his face. How could you learn to know and adore every bit of a man's face in just a few days? The high cheekbones that gave him a touch of arrogance; the wings of dark hair above his ears; the tiny lines that fanned out beside his eyes; the fine, sculptured line of his lips. He was so close that she could recognise the individual smell of his skin. She saw the little pulse beating in his throat and her own pulses leapt wildly in response.

'Yes,' she whispered. 'Yes, it would.'

The blue eyes darkened and glowed, and his voice was deep and a little unsteady as he said, 'That's all I wanted to know.' And he took her hands and drew her to her feet as Janet came back into the room.

CHAPTER NINE

'I JUST couldn't believe it.' Janet's quirky little smile turned upon her daughter as they all sat at a corner table at Mario's a very short time later. 'I was pushing my trolley along from Customs, wondering whether I was going to manage to get a taxi, when I saw this tall, dark, handsome stranger on the other side of the barrier, among the chauffeurs, toting a huge placard announcing "FLEUR'S MOTHER" in great black letters. I thought I was dreaming.' Her soft brown eyes sent a conspiratorial look towards Eliot, who was leaning back in his chair looking extremely pleased with life.

'You see——' he took over the explanation '—you hadn't ever mentioned your mother's married name, Fleur darling, so when I'd found out the flight she would probably be on and decided to meet her and give you a surprise, that was the only way I could think of to identify myself. A very bright idea, don't you agree?' he added smugly.

'So——' Janet went on '—I was so taken aback that I suppose I stopped and stared, and he stared back and then we both began to laugh. It was a funny sort of introduction. He said, "I'm Eliot, and Fleur's waiting for us at my flat, and I'm so very glad to make your acquaintance."' She chuckled. 'It wasn't until we were in his car that he told me that you two had decided to get married. I haven't the faintest idea what I said.'

176

'You said, "Oh, really."' Eliot put in. 'Such enthusiasm!' Another smile was exchanged.

Fleur was listening to this two-sided conversation in a bemused way. She was taking in the wonderful fact that her mother and Eliot had managed to get on to happily affectionate terms right from the start—just as she had managed to do with Geoffrey. She was also slowly digesting the bewildering fact that, whatever had happened about Melissa, Eliot was quite determined to go ahead with marrying her—Fleur. And that he seemed very happy with the prospect. More than happy—he was like a great purring jungle animal after a satisfying meal.

Presumably he would fill in the details of his afternoon later. Until then she was content to eat Mario's exotic pasta and drink several glasses of Mario's deliciously heady red wine, and bask in the way that Eliot's eyes constantly returned to her face. He touched her hand, her arm, her shoulder, as if he couldn't bear to separate himself from her, and his smile was the smile of a lover. She smiled back at him dizzily.

He was drawing Janet out about her holiday in the US and she was chatting away happily. Everyone, it seemed to Fleur, was quite euphoric. Perhaps, she thought hazily, she had died and gone to heaven. There was this lovely floaty feeling that she might have been borne on angel's wings. She wanted to tell Eliot about it, but she couldn't think of the right words. Undoubtedly she had drunk far too much wine, on top of the brandy he had given her in the flat.

At last reality broke through. Eliot said, 'Darling, we're going to put Janet on the train at Paddington—

she has a seat booked on the night train back to Cornwall. Do you feel up to walking back to the car?'

Fleur pulled her thoughts together with an effort. 'You're going home tonight, Mum? I thought some-how——'

Janet was gathering her handbag and loose coat busily. 'Oh, yes, dear, I want to get back as soon as I can. There's the shop, you know, and I must make contact with your Mrs Black, Eliot, and I'm longing to get into harness again. We're all going to be together very soon for the wedding—Eliot will tell you all the plans he's making.'

The short walk back to the Embankment, where the breeze was blowing freshly off the river, helped to clear Fleur's head. By the time Eliot had got the car out of the garage and driven to Paddington, she was feeling almost normal.

'I'll just check your reservation if you'll let me have the tickets,' Eliot said, and left Fleur and her mother alone on the station forecourt.

'He's being tactful, love,' Janet said. 'What a *very* nice man he is.' Her brown eyes were misty as she kissed Fleur, holding her tight. 'It's all been so quick and sur-prising that I haven't quite taken it in yet, but I've got a feeling in my bones that you're going to be very happy.'

'And you are too, aren't you, Mum?'

Janet grinned her cheerful little grin, the grin that re-minded Fleur of all the years of struggle when her mother's optimism had taken them through the ups and downs of her own growing-up days. 'Of course I'll be happy,' Janet said, as if there weren't any doubt about it. 'Won't I have a super shop? And Eliot was telling me about tentative plans his father has to join a sort of family venture. It all sounds most exciting.'

Eliot returned and handed back the tickets. 'I hope you don't mind, Janet,' he said rather tentatively. 'I've taken the liberty of changing your booking to a first-class cabin. You'll find it more comfortable—and it's just my way of saying thank you for putting up with me.'

Janet reached up and kissed his cheek. 'Thank *you*, Eliot. I'd put up with more than that for the luxury of first-class travel,' she laughed as they all walked along the platform together, searching for her compartment.

The train was not due to leave for over an hour, so goodbyes were said and Eliot drove slowly back to Chelsea and garaged the car.

He took Fleur's arm and led her across the wide street to the riverside. They stood leaning on the parapet, looking down at the black swell of water swishing gently against the walls of the Embankment. Lights twinkled all along the South Bank opposite. The dark shadow of a barge moved slowly down river, skirting the buoys that bobbed and swayed. Somewhere a night bird that had chosen city life squawked loudly. Cars glided along behind them almost silently.

'I love this part of London at night,' Eliot said. 'There's something about it—oh, I don't know—almost mysterious. It's funny, isn't it——' he turned her round to face him '—that we've spent days beside the blue, romantic Mediterranean, and yet I've got to come back to dear, grimy old London to tell you how much I love you.'

Fleur's heart began to thud. 'But—Melissa?'

A little smile touched Eliot's mouth. 'Exactly—Melissa,' he said. 'Melissa is past history now. Some time, perhaps tomorrow, I'll tell you the whole story. But for now, my darling, lovely flower-girl, is it enough to tell you I love you to distraction and I'm holding you to your promise to marry me and I'll make you fall in love with me, however long it takes? Is it enough?' He shook her gently.

'Oh, yes,' she said softly. 'It's enough. And it won't take very long. About minus a week, I'd think.'

He stared down into her eyes in silence for a long moment, taking that in. Then he said, very quietly, 'I think perhaps we'd better go back to the flat.' And, arms entwined, not speaking, they crossed the road.

The first thing Fleur heard next morning was the sound of the entry-phone buzzing in the living-room. Oh, God, she thought stupidly, *Melissa has come back.*

Eliot's arm was thrown round her, heavy against her ribs; he was sleeping deeply. The buzzing stopped, started again. Blinking herself awake, Fleur twisted free, slid out of bed and tottered into the next room. 'Yes?' she croaked at the instrument warily.

'Oh, is that Mrs Stevens?' a perky feminine voice, decidedly Cockney, enquired. 'This is Mrs Frost. We haven't met yet, have we? I thought you and your hubby might be home by now, so I just pressed the bell on spec. Would you like me to come up and do the rooms for you, Mrs Stevens?'

Mrs Stevens! Fleur looked down at the slim wedding ring on her left hand. Not long now, she thought, giggling a little. 'Well, perhaps not today, Mrs Frost,' she said into the instrument. 'We were very late getting home last night and my husband is still fast asleep. Perhaps if you could come tomorrow morning?'

'Righty-o, will do,' the voice responded cheerily. 'See you then.'

Fleur went back into the bedroom and sat for a long time looking at Eliot sleeping. It was true what they said—a strong man looks very vulnerable when he is asleep. Just looking at him made her throat choky, and she wanted to weep. Instead she went into the bathroom, showered, put on a black silk dressing-gown of Eliot's that she found hanging behind the door, and went into the kitchen to make tea. The quartz clock on the wall told her it was ten-fifteen. They had slept for nearly eleven hours.

She carried the tray back to the bedroom and slipped into bed beside Eliot. The clink of the cups must have disturbed him, for he opened his eyes with a grunt and muttered, 'Tea, for the love of Mike.'

She poured him a cup and watched with a little smile while he dragged himself up sufficiently to take a long swig of the hot, reviving liquid. After that he was awake immediately. He put down his cup on the bedside-table and smiled beautifully at her and said, 'Fleur—good morning, my darling,' and reached out and pulled her against him and nuzzled his head into the warmth of her breast.

'You feel wonderful,' he sighed. 'All soft and cuddly. Last night wasn't enough—I want to make love to you again.'

'Again?' she teased, pretending to look puzzled. 'We didn't make love last night.'

He lifted his head, frowning. 'We didn't? But—but——' He looked baffled. 'What happened—oh, God—couldn't I——?'

Fleur was laughing at him. 'You got into bed and you were dead to the world in two minutes flat. Not surprising, when you'd had hardly any sleep for thirty-six hours!'

'I—see.' A slow grin pulled at his mouth. 'Well, I'm not sleepy now. I have a sort of memory that last night you said you loved me. I didn't dream it, did I? And why, for Pete's sake, have you got that dressing-gown on?' He began to ease it off her shoulders expertly.

The warmth of his body against hers was druggingly sweet. Her lids drooped lazily over green eyes that grew soft and misty as a slow, rising rapture took over her whole body.

'No, you didn't dream it, my darling,' she told him, loving him with her eyes, as her hands began to pass gently over the smooth skin of his arms, tangled in the dark hair of his chest, stroked down over his flat stomach, over his strongly muscled thighs. He lay very still as she explored his body, but she heard the way his breathing quickened as she drew nearer to the vital centre of his maleness.

Nothing like this had happened to Fleur before—she acted from instinct, feminine instinct that needed to give as well as receive pleasure, and as he suddenly cried out sharply she knew that her instinct hadn't failed.

'Oh, God, Fleur. Wonderful—marvellous!' He was shivering as his mouth came down to hers in a deep, demanding kiss, and she kissed him back with rising passion as their tongues met and entwined. At the same moment his hand closed over her breast and she, in her turn, cried out with delight.

It was a slowly rising tide of loving, not the wild passion of that night in France, both of them timing their caresses to wring the last exquisite drop of rapture from their joining together. Only at the end did an intense, overwhelming passion take over, and they moved together as one, Eliot's head buried in Fleur's shoulder, her own head thrown back as her body arched against his in plunging, violent need, and she cried out his name as the great wave rose, broke and ebbed slowly away and they lay still, drained and gasping.

At last Eliot rolled the weight of his body off her and his breathing returned to normal. He lifted himself on one elbow and looked down into Fleur's face and smoothed back the damp strands of tawny hair from her forehead. 'That,' he said huskily, 'was a revelation. I didn't know it could be like that.'

She reached up and touched his stubbly chin. 'Me, too,' she said.

'And to think,' he mused, 'that we have the rest of our lives to practise how to make it even better.'

'Impossible!' she giggled weakly.

'You wait and see,' he promised.

Fleur lay and looked up at the ceiling. It was papered in palest blue with a pattern of darker blue interlacing circles. She studied it in detail for a few minutes of silence and then she said, 'Eliot—what happened yesterday afternoon? Or would you rather not tell me?'

'Of course I'll tell you—we mustn't start by having secrets.'

He was silent for a while, collecting his thoughts, and then he went on evenly, 'Melissa was in rather a state, and when I'd dried her tears and we'd driven to the nearest parking meter, she told me that she'd run away from her mother in Cornwall and come to London to be with her father. Apparently their marriage is on the verge of breaking up, and she thought her father would understand her better. It seems that he did and she's been living with him—and his current mistress—at an apartment in St John's Wood all week. That's where I delivered her after she'd unburdened herself to me. Her father's going to send her to Switzerland, to a sort of finishing school for young ladies, and she seems to think she'll like that. But she badly wanted to contact me before she left—she feels guilty for the way she behaved and I think she just wanted to say she was sorry and know I'd forgiven her.'

He shook his head.

'Poor child, it wasn't her fault. It was that mother of hers, who should have been in the care of a psychologist years ago. Melissa didn't have a chance to grow up. You see, her mother had brought her up like a princess in a fairy-tale. She never allowed her to go to school, or to parties, among all those nasty coarse boys.' He grimaced. 'She had a private governess until she was eighteen. Her friends were hand-picked, and Mama was always hovering to see what was going on. She told me all this as we sat in the car, and it explained a great deal. Mama was terrified that her lovely, pure, innocent daughter would be corrupted. All she wanted was to get her married to some solid citizen—like me, heaven help me. She pushed Melly into the engagement and I, poor fool, was so struck dumb by the girl's beauty that I didn't realise what the score was. We didn't have time to get to know each other before the marriage was upon us—arranged by Mama, of course, who couldn't wait to get the knot tied. It was like some Victorian novel. I realised that Melissa was—shy and innocent. That was the way I thought of it and I was gentle with her. But she wasn't only innocent—she was completely ignorant. She knew nothing of men and marriage, nothing at all. Then, of course, came the moment of truth. The day before the wedding, when I took her out to lunch, I lost my head rather and scared the wits out of her. I saw what had happened and apologised, of course. I thought it would all come right after we were married—although I was beginning to wonder——'

He paused so long that Fleur thought the tale was ended, but at last he went on, 'When it came to the wedding, she knew she couldn't go through with getting married. Her father was waiting downstairs to take her to the church and she panicked. She pulled off her wedding-dress, got into jeans and a jumper, and escaped down the back stairs and down to the beach somehow, without being seen—all the servants were at the church. She wandered about there for hours before they finally found her. I'll leave you to imagine what Mama said. And that, Fleur darling, is the whole story.'

Fleur said slowly. 'You loved her very much.'

'Yes, I loved her. I fell in love with a dream of beauty, as men often do, but the dream hadn't any substance. I knew yesterday that the dream was dead.' He smiled rather sadly. 'Yesterday, I think I could have persuaded her to marry me—if I'd still wanted to.'

'But you didn't want to?' Fleur said in a very small voice.

He turned to her, and his eyes were brilliantly blue and there was a blaze of tenderness shining there that took her breath away. 'My darling girl,' he said. 'I've found myself a real woman. What would I want with a child bride?'

He bent his head and kissed her temple, where the bright hair grew away. 'I guessed what was happening to me almost as soon as we got to Italy,' he said. 'I wanted to make sure of you, but you wouldn't have it and—and I suppose I'd lost my nerve, after all that had happened. I resolved to play it very cool until the right moment came. I thought you were responding to me, in spite of your reservations. Then, on the way home, it came together, didn't it? *We* came together. After that, I couldn't get you back to London quickly enough to make it all legal.'

He rubbed his cheek against her hair. 'Any questions?' he smiled.

'Only one,' Fleur said dreamily. 'How much do you love me?'

'You're the whole of my life and you always will be, my little flower-girl,' he said in a low, husky voice. 'I haven't the words to tell you. But I could show you,' he added. 'Shall I?'

'Yes,' whispered Fleur, turning into his arms. 'Oh, yes.'

Some time later they got up and made breakfast and carried it back to bed on trays. Eliot was full of plans, as usual.

'We should be able to arrange our wedding for Friday,' he said, and added a little anxiously, 'You won't mind having a civil wedding? Somehow I don't think I could quite tackle another wait at the altar.' He smiled ruefully, and as she saw that smile Fleur knew that at last it was really over for him—the memory and the pain.

'I won't mind,' she assured him. 'When we go to Porthgurran I'd like to visit our little vicar there. He's a sweetie—I'm sure he'd be delighted to give us his blessing.'

'That,' agreed Eliot, 'is a very good idea.'

He went on planning. 'A quiet wedding,' he said. 'I'd like Toby and Mandy to be there. Your mother, of course. And I think Mrs Black should be invited—she's been a great help. We'll have a lunch somewhere, and when we get back to Porthgurran we can lay on a little party for your friends there. How does that sound?'

'Super,' said Fleur dreamily. She would happily leave all the planning to him—for the time being at least!

'And for tonight,' Eliot went on, 'I shall take you out to dinner to the most expensive, glittering restaurant I can manage to book a table at. I want to show you off to all the men who will be as jealous as hell when they see my beautiful wife—well, nearly my wife.'

'Sounds marvellous,' Fleur agreed. 'Eliot—'

'Yes, my love?'

She looked thoughtful. 'We're going out to dinner at a posh restaurant, you said?'

'That's the idea, sweetheart.'

The green eyes were suddenly dreamy. '*Very* posh?'

'Top people,' he grinned, his hand stroking her shoulder absently.

A small dimple appeared in Fleur's cheek. 'Then——' she said, 'there's this dress I'll be wearing—one that you haven't seen yet—a very, very romantic kind of dress——'

COMING IN JUNE

Janet DAILEY

THE MASTER FIDDLER

Jacqui didn't want to go back to college, and she didn't
want to go home. Tombstone, Arizona, wasn't in her
plans, either, until she found herself stuck there en route
to L.A. after ramming her car into rancher Choya Barnett's
Jeep. Things got worse when she lost her wallet and
couldn't pay for the repairs. The mechanic wasn't
interested when she practically propositioned him to get
her car back—but Choya was. He took care of her bills and
then waited for the debt to be paid with the only thing
Jacqui had to offer—her virtue.

Watch for this bestselling Janet Dailey favorite, coming in
June from Harlequin.

Also watch for *Something Extra* in August and *Sweet
Promise* in October.

ANNOUNCING . . .

The Lost Moon Flower
by Bethany Campbell

**Look for it this August
wherever Harlequins are sold**

HR 3000-1

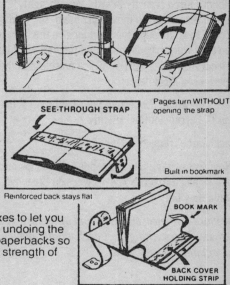

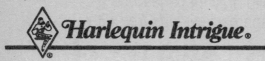

They went in through the terrace door. The house was dark, most of the servants were down at the circus, and only Nelbert's hired security guards were in sight. It was child's play for Blackheart to move past them, the work of two seconds to go through the solid lock on the terrace door. And then they were creeping through the darkened house, up the long curving stairs, Ferris fully as noiseless as the more experienced Blackheart.

They stopped on the second floor landing. "What if they have guns?" Ferris mouthed silently.

Blackheart shrugged. "Then duck."

"How reassuring," she responded. Footsteps directly above them signaled that the thieves were on the move, and so should they be.

For more romance, suspense and adventure, read Harlequin Intrigue. Two exciting titles each month, available wherever Harlequin Books are sold.